A Hellish Highlander

Clan Ross
Book Three

Hildie McQueen

ARE YOU SIGNED UP FOR DRAGONBLADE'S BLOG?

You'll get the latest news and information on exclusive giveaways, exclusive excerpts, coming releases, sales, free books, cover reveals and more.

Check out our complete list of authors, too!

No spam, no junk. That's a promise!

Sign Up Here

www.dragonbladepublishing.com

Dearest Reader;

Thank you for your support of a small press. At Dragonblade Publishing, we strive to bring you the highest quality Historical Romance from the some of the best authors in the business. Without your support, there is no 'us', so we sincerely hope you adore these stories and find some new favorite authors along the way.

Happy Reading!

CEO, Dragonblade Publishing

Additional Dragonblade books by Author Hildie McQueen

Clan Ross Series
A Heartless Laird
A Hardened Warrior
A Hellish Highlander
A Flawed Scotsman
A Fearless Rebel

The Lyon's Den Connected World
The Lyon's Laird

PROLOGUE

*K*IERAN ROSS, THIRD-BORN *son to Robert and Madeline Ross, often traveled with his father to check on the people who lived in the outlying lands.*

Little did they expect on this unremarkable day that the actions of madman would change their lives forever.

THE HOWLING SCREAM pierced Kieran Ross almost as if it were he who was sliced open with the sharp sword.

His father's bewildered expression, wide-open eyes and gaping mouth would be forever etched in Kieran's mind.

With hands outstretched toward Kieran, Robert Ross fell to the ground, his guts spilling out onto the dirt, twisting and spreading like live snakes.

The sounds of horses whinnying, swords clanging and screams all faded as Kieran collapsed onto the soil, his knees faltering, no longer holding him upright.

"Father…no! No!" Kieran cried out, clutching his father's face, willing him to live.

Somehow, strength kept the injured man conscious enough to speak. "Help me…not like this…not like this." His father gasped out each word, fear evident in his tear-filled eyes. "I do not wish to die. Help me…Son."

It wasn't possible that his father was cut down in front of him and he didn't stop the aggressor, or defend him. How could it be that the guards who flanked the laird not see it coming? How could everyone have been so blind? So very reckless?

"We will get ye home. Our healer will take care of ye. Do not give up," Kieran said, believing every word. "Look at me," he demanded when his father's gaze moved upward. "Father, look at me."

"I do not want to die," his father repeated, this time softer. "Help me, Son." The injured man's grip on Kieran's tunic loosened.

Kieran shook his father with force. "Father!"

The laird's gaze met his once again. He attempted to say something, but no sound came out. Desperation filled Kieran and he screamed. "Look at me."

His father's gaze did not move, but remained fixed on the sky. Again his mouth moved, mimicking a fish out of water.

"Father?"

Boots came into view. "Kieran, we have a cart. Let us take him to the healer."

Whoever the man was gave Kieran hope and he lifted his father up, causing the contents of his midsection to spill out more.

The smell was horrendous as some of the contents of his bowels had leaked, but Kieran ignored it.

Desperation poured out of every part of him as he lowered his father to the ground and began scooping the insides back into the almost empty cavity. "Do not stand there. Help me," he growled.

"It is no use, he's gone," someone, perhaps the same guard, said.

"No he is not," Kieran screamed, looking up at his father's still face. "He is not."

When someone placed a hand on his shoulder, it felt as if they seared his skin with a red poker and he jerked away. Continuing in what seemed an almost impossible task, he continued to push blood and guts back into his father, his bloody hands becoming crusted with dirt and straw from the ground.

Once it seemed completed, he scrambled to take his father's face in his hands. "Father, can ye hear me?"

"We must load him onto the cart," someone said and Kieran looked up to see an old farmer, a friend to his father. "Take him home, Son."

Kieran pulled his father against his chest as an animalistic howl erupted. He could not stop, each hoarse cry filling the air like the sounds of an injured beast.

Whether his father was taken from him or he was the one to carry him to the cart, Kieran wouldn't recall. All he knew was that his life was forever changed and there would be no peace within him until the man who'd cut his father's life short died by his own hand.

Kieran Ross would not rest or be distracted from what, in that moment, became the most important quest of his life.

He would make the bastard who killed his father pay for what he did.

Ethan McLeod would pay tenfold for the actions of that day.

CHAPTER ONE

I T SEEMED HIS enemy would live another day.

Kieran Ross slipped sideways, his head tilting to the side and he almost fell off his steed. After two full days on horseback, it was impossible to continue.

He tried to ride nonstop to the northern post, but the trip that would normally take a week was much too far to do so without stopping to sleep and rest. Laith, his horse, was also exhausted and had slowed to a slow trudge for hours.

When a familiar village came into view, he urged Laith forward. It was idiotic to continue. If he ran into his nemesis at this point, it was doubtful he'd be able to muster enough energy to lift his sword.

Seeming to sense the possibility of food and rest, his horse picked up the pace and, within minutes, they arrived at the small village on Munro lands.

Clan Munro and Kieran's own clan were to be united, as his sister, Verity, and their mother would travel there in a couple of days. Verity was set to marry the eldest of the Munro's sons.

The village stables were clean and well maintained, so he did not hesitate to board his steed there.

The instability of Kieran's legs reinforced, the decision to stop was a good one and he ambled to a tavern in hopes of a hot meal and a warm bed.

It was early evening, so when he entered the tavern, it was not surprising that only one table remained empty. Thankfully, it was near a window, so he could keep an eye out in the distant possibility the bastard he sought would happen upon the village as well.

A wench neared and he let out an annoyed breath. First her eyes would widen, and then she'd take a couple beats to formulate words. Hopefully, she'd not ask his name or any other bothersome things.

The woman walked over, her gaze barely touching on him before she looked past him to the window.

Ever so slowly, she looked back to him and she gasped. Not seeming to care that he took notice of what she did, her hand came over her chest. Slowing her progress, she approached slowly as if he would disappear at any moment.

"Wh…What can I get for ye?" she asked in a breathless voice, her gaze roaming over his face. "Are ye staying the night?"

Interesting combination of words this time he considered. "Ale and whatever stew ye have, bread…"

"Oh, of course, right away," she interrupted. "Anything else?" The woman leaned forward, ensuring he got a clear view of her ample bosom. "At all?"

He gave her a flat, bored look. Much too tired to care, he shook his head. "Just a bed for the night."

Lips curving, she hurried away and he groaned. Did she think he'd said it because of what she obviously offered? When she returned, he'd make sure to clear things up.

Not much later, stomach full, he trudged up the steps to a room. The woman downstairs watched him with obvious dejection until the barkeep shoved her sideways. "Stop yer gawking and see about cleaning the tables."

Once inside the small, but clean room, Kieran collapsed onto the bed fully clothed. The last time he'd come through this village, it had earned him a scratched face from a beautiful soap seller he'd propositioned. Both were a first for him, the proposition and the rebuttal.

He was overly aware his attractive face brought excessive attention. However, the scar from the scratch across his cheek was proof that not all women were quick to bed with him because of his looks. He actually wished the scar would remain.

The incident had been his fault. Not used to rejection, he'd been shocked by the quick and very decisive rebuff. Not only had a pretty lass been shocked at his crude proposition, but also slapped him across the face, hard, her sharp nails leaving a lasting reminder of his lack of decorum.

The scar had healed, but the mark from it, although faint, still remained. His lips curved remembering the narrowed dark brown eyes blazing with fury that had met his.

"Leave at once and take yer money," she had screamed and thrown his coins at him. The soap seller had refused to sell to him. Thinking back on it, he didn't blame her.

This day, it had been too late when he'd arrived for any sellers to be in the town square. Not that he would have had the energy to stop and search for the lass.

Kieran's eyes popped wide. Why was he thinking about a woman? Ever since Ethan McLeod had killed his father, the only thing he'd thought about day after day was revenge.

Vengeance motivated his every movement, the need for it fueling his every breath. Now was not the time to allow a woman to distract him from the goal.

Ethan McLeod was mad and had no regard for the harm his actions cost his own clan or others. It could be that because of his madness that he was so hard to find and track. The last the Ross scouts had found out was that Ethan was headed north.

News of Kieran having been assigned to the northern post had probably reached the idiot and he'd headed north in an effort to hunt him down.

Interesting, his prey thought himself to be the hunter. In this case, Kieran mused, both played equal parts, hunter and prey.

Thoughts of a woman would have to be pushed away. He would rest and sleep until his body decided to rise. Then after a robust meal, he would continue his trek north. From the village, it was only half a day's ride to the northern post. But he would take his time. If by some chance Ethan had slowed to plan for an attack, it was best to be cautious.

With a plan in mind and a route mapped out, Kieran let out a breath and allowed exhaustion to carry him to slumber. However, dark brown eyes reappeared, and he grunted. Fine. He'd allow the fantasy, but only because fighting it would make it harder to fall asleep.

And so with pictures of the brunette beauty he'd met in the market, Kieran fell into a deep slumber.

LIGHT HIT HIS face and he realized the sun was already high in the sky as he sat up the next morning. Kieran stretched, feeling rested and ready to head out.

In the tavern, there was only the barkeep and an older woman, who served him without too much annoyance. Although the woman noticed him, she maintained a cool demeanor.

After a good meal, he walked out of the tavern and headed for the stables. Unable to keep from it, he looked to the town square where sellers called out, hoping to get attention. A few people milled about inspecting the wares displayed. He didn't spot the soap vendor and let out a breath.

Good. Kieran ignored the slight tinge of disappointment.

Once mounted, he guided Laith from the village and out to an open field that spread between the village and Munro Keep that stood atop a slight hill.

The day was perfect for the long ride ahead, the light breeze blowing across his face made for deep inhales. However, not prone to such idiotic displays, Kieran grunted and urged Laith to a faster trot.

In the distance, a woman raced across the field toward Munro Keep. Holding her skirts up past her knees, she ran as if the devil himself chased after her. Scanning the surroundings, there was no one else. Kieran could tell she wasn't being pursued.

She didn't slow or look back but it was certain she was in some sort of distress. Kieran slowed his horse, not quite sure what to make of the scene before him.

Suddenly she disappeared. Having tripped over something, she went down to the ground and, just as quickly, scrambled up, stumbled a couple steps and then once again began running.

"What is wrong with that woman?" Kieran asked Laith whose ears twitched. "I agree, none of my business."

As he progressed further, he and the woman would come closer. Deciding to ignore her, he and Laith continued.

"Ye!" she shouted, pointing at Kieran. "Help me."

Kieran looked behind, hoping someone else was about. There wasn't time for dramatics. It wasn't the woman from the tavern, however, it was possible this woman had heard of his presence and sought a pretext to speak to him.

Unable to ignore her, he urged Laith closer. "What do ye want? I haven't the time for hysterics." Ensuring a bored look, he peered down at the woman.

Both of their eyes widened in recognition. It was the woman from the village, none other than the soap seller.

She recovered first and scowled up at him. "Ye."

Not exactly a response he was accustomed to, especially from a young woman. But then again, she had slapped and scratched his face the last time they'd met.

Kieran sneered. "Aye, me. And ye find yerself in need of assistance?"

Looking toward the keep, she seemed to consider running again, but then looked back at him. Face flushed and chest lifting and lowering from her ordeal, she was breathtaking.

"Can ye please take me to the keep? Just to the gates. I must get there. Tis a matter of life or death."

The keep was not so much of a distance that it would delay him by more than a few minutes. So finally, he nodded. "Very well. However, do not expect more than for me to lower ye to the ground and leave. I will not escort ye in."

The woman blew out a breath and rolled her eyes. "I do not require it. If my mother had not taken my horse and cart, I wouldn't require yer assistance at all."

With that statement, she lifted her hands so he could help her up. Once she was seated before him, both of them fell silent.

Kieran urged his mount forward and guided it toward the keep.

He had questions. Why was the woman in such a hurry? What caused the urgency? But deciding the less he knew the easier to forget the episode, he kept quiet.

It was the first time he'd held a woman in his arms in this manner. Not one for romanticisms, he'd never offered a lass to ride with him. As a matter of fact, he preferred no complications when it came to the fairer sex. A tryst was fine. Anything more than that was a bother.

She shifted and he became aware of her soft curves touching him. Her bottom was against his sex and he gritted his teeth at the reaction it caused. She smelled fresh; a sweet fragrance like that of flowers or fruit.

It must be the soap she made.

Unable to keep from it, he sniffed her hair.

"Did ye just smell my hair?" She threw him a piercing look over her shoulder. "Stop sniffing me."

"Then ye should not keep flinging it about," he snapped. "Twice, yer hair has blown across my face."

She grabbed the loose tendrils and pulled them in front of her shoulder. "Ye may come to my stand and choose a soap or two for yer trouble."

"I am not planning to return to yer village."

She shrugged. "Then I am unable to repay ye."

"Will the Munro allow ye in?" Kieran studied the keep gates as they grew closer. The gates were closed and guards stood watch.

The lass did the same, craning her neck to look up. The action made her lean back against his chest. "My late father and the laird are brothers..." she left off and sighed. "I am a Munro."

Kieran remained silent, not wishing to continue conversing, instead becoming anxious for her to be gone. Every moment that passed, he was beginning to wish she'd not move away. That her soft body would continue to remain between his thighs, her bottom pressed against his sex and her back against his chest.

It was a natural reaction, of course. It had little to do with her. Whoever this niece of the Munro was, she was a nuisance and nothing more.

As they arrived at the gates, once again she leaned against him and looked up. "Tis me, Gisela Munro. Allow me in."

"Who are ye?" A guard pointed at Kieran.

"I am Kieran Ross. I am not entering," he shouted back.

"Open the gates!" the guard called down.

"Down with ye," Kieran said as he took her by the waist.

Gisela swung her leg around and allowed him to lower her. She peered up at him. "Thank ye." Her upper lip curved just a bit. "This almost redeems ye for the horrible remark ye made the last time our paths crossed."

"Kieran Ross." A man stood just inside the gates. Whoever he was, he ignored Gisela as she raced past him and headed to the house. "Ye must come and speak to my father."

Kieran didn't recognize the man and he started to make an excuse for the offer and turn away.

Then he recalled an archery competition. The man, Caylen Munro, the laird's second born, had been one of his fiercest competitors. Unfortunately, he was also a pompous ass.

"I must go. I have duties at our northern guard post."

"A messenger came and left word for ye," the man persisted

while turning and allowing his gaze to follow Gisela as she made her way into the house. "Seems yer family was a wee bit delayed."

Irritated at a second interruption, Kieran dismounted and stalked into the courtyard, pulling Laith forward. When lads hurried over to look after the horse, he stopped. "Ensure ye keep his saddle where I can find it. He will be grateful for water and oats."

Caylen walked alongside Kieran, making absolutely no effort to show his impatience. "I must go see about something," Caylen said and hesitated upon them entering the great room. His gaze scanned the room until he found Gisela, who spoke with an older woman.

"I do not require escort," Kieran replied, not liking at all how Caylen ogled Gisela. However, he had no claim on the woman and perhaps the two knew each other and had plans.

A servant neared and Caylen waved toward a corridor. "Escort him to see my father." The man then hurried toward where Gisela was standing.

"I am Kieran Ross," Kieran told the confused servant.

Laird Munro was a short man with a bushy beard and a loud voice. The few times Kieran had met him, he'd always seemed in good spirits. Although it was interesting to note that the Munro was known for overindulging in drink, the man seemed a fair sort.

"Ah, Kieran, the youngest of the Ross brothers," Laird Munro exclaimed as Kieran entered the room. "I did not expect ye to arrive for another day or so." He motioned for Kieran to come closer. "Yer brother, Tristan, was here last. He is a good negotiator. I have yet to see yer eldest brother, Malcolm. I know taking over as laird is taxing, but he needs to make sure to meet with other lairds."

Kieran opened his mouth to speak, but the laird continued. "One must ensure relationships are formed and remain strong. Tell him that."

"I am in a hurry…"

"Oh, I bet. The warm weather makes it a perfect time to attend festivities. We plan one tonight, for which ye will be an honored guest." The laird went to a side table and poured whisky into cups. "Tis good to have guests arrive already. Ye will be glad ye came. There is much to celebrate."

Kieran wasn't sure how to respond, so he took the drink and scowled into it. "I cannot remain…"

"Yes, of course. I apologize for not getting to the point. A messenger came to let us know that yer party would be delayed and that ye would come ahead of them." The laird looked around Kieran. "Archers…more are with ye, aye?"

"They follow and will be here by tomorrow."

"Perfect," the man boomed. "Just in time for the competition. Tis always good to have men with skills such as yers to get my archers to do their best."

Confused and barely able to keep from rudely telling the man to tell him the message, Kieran nodded. "What else did the messenger state?"

The laird scratched his beard. "The lad is here. Somewhere."

"Who?"

"The messenger, of course," Laird Munro laughed. "A wee, thin lad. Probably in the kitchen eating."

Unable to keep from glowering, Kieran swallowed down the drink. "If someone would show me the way to the kitchens…"

"We shall discuss the competition at last meal," the laird said, walking out of the room with Kieran. "Clan Mackenzie is also sending a group of archers. Although I must admit, they have relied on numbers too long and, individually, they are not much of a threat when competing."

His back teeth hurt from grinding down so hard. Did the man ever stop talking long enough to hear others? "Caylen told me there was a delay in my family arriving."

"Oh, aye. The messenger said they would arrive in two or three days, which I suppose is later than was expected."

It was not a delay, but the original travel plans. Kieran wanted to hit a wall with his fist. Now he was trapped. If he declined the laird's invitation to remain and continued on his trek, it would be a great insult to the clan his family was about to unite with.

Once he spoke to the messenger to ensure there wasn't any other news, he would find Gisela. The woman would know how much of a problem she was turning out to be.

Because of bringing her to the keep, his plans were ruined.

CHAPTER TWO

"MOTHER, WE SHOULD return to the village. Tis obvious Laird Munro and his family have much to attend to and no time for us," Gisela repeated for what seemed the twentieth time.

"Caylen Munro seems quite taken by ye," her mother said with a giggle. "And he did insist we remain. It would be rude to leave."

It was more than obvious to Gisela that the only thing Caylen Munro was interested in was someone warming his bed. The man had no intentions of marrying anytime soon. The well-known rogue had a reputation for ruining many a lass in the village. Not only was he without scruples, in Gisela's opinion, but also not the sort she would ever desire in a husband.

Gisela leaned into her mother's ear. "Why would I wish to marry a man that has tupped every girl in the village? Besides, he is my cousin."

"Oh, Gisela, ye do not know that for sure. People tend to exaggerate when the laird's handsome son is in question."

Instead of arguing, she tugged at her mother's hand. "I am leaving. Do ye wish to come with me or not?"

"Oh, goodness," her mother stammered, her mouth falling

open and her eyes opening wide. "Is he an apparition? Truly, that man is not of this earth."

Immediately, Gisela knew whom her mother spoke of. She'd thought Kieran Ross would have left by now. Her initial reaction to him had been the same but, thankfully, she'd recovered by the time he'd stopped at her stand. While he'd strolled through the town square, everyone in the village had gawked, much like her mother did at the moment. Then he'd stopped at her humble stand, looked at her soaps, picked one up and sniffed and then another. Finally, his gaze lifted to hers and he held out coins. "I will take two. How much extra for a few moments of yer time?"

Without thinking of any consequence, she'd slapped him across the face so hard her palm had stung. To make matters worse, her nails had cut into his skin, leaving an angry red cut. Both she and he had been stunned silent for a few moments.

Expecting a man who was obviously highborn to hit her back, or worse drag her away by the hair, every person in the square watched with ill-concealed curiosity.

Later, Gisela would recall that a couple of men had stood at the ready to defend her, if it came to it.

He'd let out a breath, his cheek turning crimson. "I apologize," he'd said.

Apologies did not undo the lack of respect. She'd thrown the coins to the ground.

At the moment, everyone in the room tracked his every step. In a way, Gisela felt bad for him. It had to be a burden to attract so much attention no matter where he went.

Much like her mother, every other person in the room followed Kieran Ross' every movement. The conversation in the room dimmed and many craned their necks to get another look as he stalked across the room.

"He seems to be coming to speak to ye." Her mother's breathless words made Gisela cringe.

"I certainly hope not."

Kieran's hazel eyes pinned her with a not too friendly glare and Gisela looked up to the ceiling to let him know he did not intimidate her. In truth, the effect he had on her was much like she imagined he had on every woman he came across. She'd die before ever admitting it to him.

Kieran Ross was perfection. He was tall with broad shoulders, muscular and yet graceful, a body that promised to be as alluring as his face. Golden waves fell just above his shoulders, the unruly locks only adding to his attraction.

On this day, he wore a simple tunic over brown breeches that molded to his muscular legs. On his feet, he wore weathered boots.

Gisela lifted an eyebrow in question when he neared. "I thought ye were in a hurry to leave."

"Gisela!" her mother gasped. "Do not be ill-mannered."

"I was." Kieran's words came out between clenched teeth. "But ye ruined it."

"Me?" Gisela glared at him. "What did I do?"

"I am Lillian Munro, Gisela's mother," her mother interrupted, holding her hand out palm down. "And ye are?"

Taken by surprise, Kieran looked to her mother and took her hand. He did not kiss it. Instead, he gave a slight bow. "Kieran Ross."

"Oh, of course," her mother continued as if they were at a social gathering. "Yer sister is to marry Patrick, the eldest son of the Munro."

Kieran nodded, irritation and impatience evident to everyone but her mother. Gisela fought the urge to grin at his discomfort. Although he'd been kind to bring her there, it did not excuse him speaking to her in an angry tone. If he'd come there, it was because of his sister's wedding. Obviously, he was expected to remain.

"Did ye not plan to attend yer sister's wedding?" Gisela asked as he tugged her toward a corner of the room. "Where are we going?"

He looked around once they were out of her mother's earshot. "Why are ye here? I thought it was a matter of life or death."

"It is…well, almost," Gisela's chest constricted. "I cannot leave my mother alone. She plans to ask the Munro to marry me off."

The flat gaze he gave her made Gisela want to smack him. "Is that all?"

"The rest of my life will be affected. It is very crucial that we stop her."

"We?" He snorted air out of his nose. "Be with care." Kieran started to walk away but her mother intercepted his path.

"Are ye in search of a wife, Kieran Ross?" She pronounced his name while looking over him as if he were a delicacy on a platter.

If only the ground would open up and swallow her, Gisela would be grateful at that moment.

"He is not."

"I am not."

Both spoke at the same time and exchanged matching narrow-eyed looks.

When Lady Munro came toward them, Gisela searched for a way to escape. However, at the moment, perhaps it was best to remain and ensure her mother did not do anything that would prove irreparable.

She could not marry him.

Like every woman there, Gisela realized he was breathtakingly handsome, the most attractive man she'd ever seen. However, marriage to a man who looked like Kieran Ross would mean putting up with other women constantly ogling him. Besides, he didn't seem at all the marrying type, much too broody or angry.

Lady Munro stopped when Kieran bowed at her and a smile split her face. "I just learned ye are here. I will arrange for a bedchamber." The woman stopped speaking and looked to Gisela's mother.

"Goodness, Lillian, I was not aware ye were here," Lady Munro gushed and returned her attention to Kieran. "We have much to do to prepare for yer sister's arrival."

Her mother took the opportunity to secure an invitation. "It is precisely why we came, to help where we can. We are family after all."

Lady Munro and her mother were much alike. Both acted half their age and talked nonstop. "How wonderful," Lady Munro replied and looked to Gisela. "And to bring my niece as well."

No. No. No. It could not be happening. Gisela looked to Kieran who started to walk away toward the front door.

"I cannot possibly stay. I'd only be in the way…" Gisela started.

"Ye should stay," Kieran said.

Gisela fought not to glare at him. Why did he remain there? Surely he had things to tend to. "Should ye not look after yer horse or something?"

"Of course ye will remain here. There is plenty of room." Lady Munro motioned to the already overfilled space. "I am sure…" she finished weakly, seeming to notice for the first time how overcrowded the great room was. "Goodness, who are all these people?"

She headed off in a hurry.

When Gisela turned to see what Kieran was doing, he was already near the front door. She eyed the doorway, considering that perhaps with so many people about, it would be easy to make an escape.

"Do not think about leaving. Ye heard Lady Munro. She requires our assistance."

"I am sure she does not," Gisela told her mother.

A loud banging got everyone's attention. A man she recognized as a member of the council stood at the high board hitting a metal plate with a spoon. "Everyone must go. The room has to be prepared for a family gathering. If ye require anything of Laird Munro, he will be hearing ye outside in the side courtyard."

Slowly, the people began dispersing. Gisela grabbed her mother's arm. "Ye heard the man. Let us go."

Her mother was stronger than expected as she fought Gisela's tugs to the doorway. "Surely he did not mean us," Lillian argued.

Gisela managed to tug her mother to the door. Once outside, her mother hurried to a group of four women who spoke animatedly. Upon nearing, her mother immediately began speaking to them, her hands motioning to Gisela. The women looked to her with approval, nodding and smiling.

Afraid to be drawn in to the conversation, but needing to fetch her mother, Gisela walked to the group.

"...too handsome for words."

"...have never seen such a face."

"...notice how he walked?"

It was obvious whom they spoke of. One of the women looked to her and grinned. "By the way he looked at ye, he has courting in mind."

Another woman fanned her face. "Have ye kissed the beautiful man?"

"Mother..." Gisela wasn't sure what to say, so she took her mother's hand. "We should leave. There is much to tend to."

They walked a few feet away and, once again, her mother stopped. "Why are ye being so difficult? I worry about ye, Gisela. Alone in the forest, anything could happen. What about when that horrible man came and left ye for dead."

Her mother was right in that the experience had been horrific. Just a few days earlier, a mad man had barged in and held her captive overnight. When she'd fought off his advances, he'd shoved her to the ground, knocking her unconscious. Although he'd not taken advantage of her, it could have easily happened.

Gisela shuddered at recalling the incident. "I know, Mother, that is why I am staying with ye until I come up with a solution."

"Marriage is the solution," her mother insisted. "Ye are almost past the age for it. Soon, no man will have ye as it will be hard for ye to carry bairns."

"I wish to marry a man of my choice." Gisela met her mother's gaze, hoping her plea worked. "Please, Mother."

Her mother turned to the courtyard, which was emptying as people left. "Then choose and do so quickly. I will be speaking to the laird. As yer uncle, he is responsible for finding ye a good husband."

Gisela sighed. "Very well."

It was best to agree with her mother. Otherwise, Lillian would dig her heels in and become overzealous in whatever her mind was set on.

"That is a good girl. Now, how about him?" Her mother pointed to a man preparing his horse. He appeared to be about thirty and he looked like he was in a hurry.

"He is the farmer who lives just outside the village. He has a wife and several bairns. Do ye not recognize him?"

Her mother leaned forward, squinting. "Oh, aye. Now I do. I do not care for his wife."

"Mother!" Gisela waited to make eye contact. "I promise to find a suitable husband. But give me at least two days to do so."

"Very well," her mother replied and hurried back to the gossiping circle.

Gisela looked around the area noticing there were plenty of guardsmen and other males who worked there. Surely there was someone that she would not mind marrying.

None took her notice and she considered the men back at the village. There was one who'd actively pursued her, but she disliked the way he treated his horse. In her opinion, a man who mistreated an animal, which he depended on, was not a good person.

She'd often gone to see about the poor creature that remained hitched to a wagon day and night. Often, the animal roamed about the village seeking food with the wagon in tow.

When she'd unhitched it once and feed it fruit, the poor thing had been ecstatic. That man was definitely not an option for a possible husband. The only reason she'd marry him would be to look after the horse.

Kieran stalked back toward the keep, his gaze forward, not

seeming to take notice of anyone around him. Possibly, it was his way so he could ignore the looks he often garnered.

However, Gisela had a distinct impression he saw everything and took notice of his surroundings.

CHAPTER THREE

THE MUNRO AND his council sat on chairs in a smaller courtyard on the side of the keep facing craggy hills. The men spoke over each other, making it impossible to understand what was being said. Those gathered waited patiently, not particularly paying the loud council much attention, which lead Kieran to believe the chaos must be a regular occurrence.

"Gentlemen." Laird Munro held both hands up. "I have made a decision. We will go forth and hold the archery competition outside the keep walls."

With only a few grumbles, the men quieted.

"Now, I must see to clan business." Laird Munro motioned a man in tattered clothes to come forward.

The man stated his situation, citing a need for provisions for his family after being run off by a landowner. The laird sent him off with a guard to be given food and clean clothing.

Kieran had to admit the proceedings gave him more respect for Malcolm, as his brother would never have allowed the man to leave without a way to earn a living and provide for his family. In addition, the Ross council rarely argued in front of the clanspeople.

It was going to be a long day as the Munro council began to

debate over a dispute between two farmers. It seemed two of them claimed the same lands and accused each other of poaching.

Not wishing to hear more of it, Kieran started to leave.

"What say ye, Kieran Ross?" the Munro called out. "In whose favor would ye rule? Who is telling the truth?" The laird motioned to the two farmers.

Kieran knew what the Munro sought. He wished for Kieran to solve the dispute impartially not having heard the facts. However, he'd been paying attention to the pair of farmers before they'd approached.

"Tis not a dispute over land space, but an ongoing family feud," Kieran started. "When there is a dispute between two families, it never ends. One day it is land, the next goats."

People laughed and the two farmers glared at each other.

"True," Laird Munro said, seeming surprised at Kieran's response. "Therefore, I find that ye each bring me a count of yer herd weekly."

"Tis too far to travel, Laird," one farmer said with a worried look. "I will lose three days…"

"Aye. I cannot come each week either," the other interrupted.

Munro shrugged. "If ye would agree that neither will take from the other, I will change it to every fortnight."

"That, too, is very often," the first farmer began.

"I tire of yer feuds. Therefore, my word stands. Every fortnight, ye will bring me a count of yer herd. If even one is unaccounted for, ye must have a good reason or the reporting will become weekly travel for ye both."

Heads down, the men walked off in silence.

Laird Munro gave Kieran a triumphant look. "Ye are quite astute."

For some strange reason, the compliment felt good.

Kieran detested situations that brought him around crowds and he wanted to ask the laird to allow him leave. He'd planned to use the overcrowding of the keep as an excuse, but now that most of the people had left, he couldn't.

Laird Munro neared. "Why did ye arrive ahead of the others?"

Deciding it was best to be honest, he met the man's gaze. "I was on my way to our northernmost post. I wished to intercept Ethan McLeod, who I believe travels there."

"Ye plan to kill him," the Laird stated, not seeming put off in the least at the idea.

"I do."

Laird Munro nodded. "Ye are within yer rights. However, I have not had any reports of him coming through or near my lands. I will see that word is spread to inform me immediately if he is spotted."

It wasn't in Kieran's nature to show emotion. Even before his father's death, he'd never been one to. Emotions got in the way of things, in Kieran's opinion. Made one too vulnerable. And yet in spite of a boisterous manner and loud laughter, Laird Munro maintained the air of a good leader.

"As soon as the handfasting is over, I will leave and continue on my quest to find that bastard."

"I believe ye will find him." The Laird became pensive. "What happens after may surprise ye."

"What do ye mean by that?"

The laird studied him for a long moment. "Sometimes when we achieve the purpose of our existence, we lose a bit of ourselves. I understand why ye seek to kill Ethan McLeod. At the same time, I wonder if it will relieve the guilt that assails ye."

Rage surged within him and Kieran let out a burst of air, as if a fist had been sunk into his gut. "I care not about what happens after Ethan's death."

When Kieran returned to the main courtyard, things had changed considerably from earlier. It was less crowded by those dispersed earlier and only a group of women remained. They spoke animatedly, their voices carrying.

Frenzied servants hauled buckets to and from the house. Bedding was being shaken from windows, which resembled tournament flags cheering competitors.

Swaying side to side, a cart full of linens entered through the gates and, immediately, servants gathered and lined up, resembling ants as they passed each other with armloads.

Preparations for his sister's wedding ceremony were in full effect and not wishing to be discourteous, Kieran decided it would be best to remain and attend. The irritation at the change in plans began to ebb. Nothing could be done about it after all.

Besides, it was only a delay. He would find Ethan McLeod and he would kill the man, whether put off by a few days or months, the vow he'd made would never change.

Before guests began arriving, it was best to find accommodations. Hopefully, he'd find a room away from the throng of people who would gather.

His features, both a curse and a blessing, garnered attention. It was good because if Ethan hunted him, the man could easily describe Kieran.

How many times had Ethan repeated "a very attractive man" when describing him? Kieran almost smiled at the thought.

Back to the present, he focused on the current irritating situation. He needed a place away from people to get some rest.

A bearded man with uncombed hair trudged from the stables to a corral with a bucket in each hand. His back rounded from the weight, he put the buckets down and opened the gate into the corral. Once inside, he emptied water into troughs.

The horses lazily meandered to the trough and sniffed, none taking the offering. The man shook his head and motioned to the animals. "'Tis fresh water, drink!"

Perfect. The stable master often had a space for someone to sleep. Kieran headed toward the corral only to stop at hearing someone call his name.

"Ross." Caylen came up, strolling as if without a care. "The archers are practicing. Would ye care to join in?"

"No." Kieran had enough of being around people for one day. "I am going to see about my horse. He had a slight limp on the way here," he lied.

The younger version of Laird Munro measured him, as if contemplating if he were telling the truth. "We are to compete in a few days. Ye may need the practice."

"Very well, I will be there shortly." Kieran wanted to shove the man away. He was a much better archer than Caylen. Today at practice, he'd allow the man to win, just barely. It would set him up for a bigger loss the day of the competition.

In the dim interior of the stables, he found Laith. His horse had his mouth buried in a bucket of oats. The animal didn't look up when he called out his name.

"Ye are greedy. If not for our travels, ye would be fat," Kieran scolded the animal that continued to ignore him. The saddle had been placed over the stable wall. From one of the saddle sacks, Kieran took out brush and ran it down Laith's side.

Laith deemed him worthy of acknowledgment and made a soft sound exclaiming his pleasure.

"Ye must speak to Mother, Hamus," a woman said. "She is going to petition the laird for a husband for me."

Gisela.

"Tis not a bad thing. I worry about ye, as well," a man replied. "Living in the cottage alone in the forest. Tis dangerous for ye, Sister."

The woman huffed. "I can take care of myself. I do not need a husband to protect me."

"What of the man who came to yer cottage? The mad one, he could have killed ye."

"But he did not. I fought him off."

"Mother found ye still as dead on the ground," the man argued. "Go on with ye. Best to find someone to yer liking before Mother choses an old troll." The man laughed at his sister's situation then a loud "oomph" sounded.

"Serves ye right for laughing at me."

Gisela stomped past the stall where Kieran remained brushing his horse. She slid him a look and rolled her eyes as she passed.

It was then that a man came into view. He was tall and slender, but the family connection was evident. He, too, had dark wavy hair and brown eyes when meeting Kieran's.

"Sisters, they are such a bother," he mumbled. "Ye have one?"

"Aye. She comes in a day to marry a Munro."

"Then ye know what a bother they can be." The man looked to Kieran. "I am Hamus. And ye must be a Ross."

Kieran walked out of the stall. "Aye, I am Kieran. Who was the man who attacked yer sister?"

Hamus shrugged. "No one she recognized. He was about our age and Gisela thinks of good social standing by his well-made clothing."

"What did he want?"

"To hide for the night. According to Gisela, he seemed exhausted. However, he was as mad as they come, babbling about killing and such."

Kieran's blood ran cold. It had to be Ethan. "When was this?"

"Almost a fortnight now."

Kieran hurried from the stables to find Gisela, but she'd disappeared. After searching the gardens and the great room, he wasn't sure where else the girl could have gone.

Finally, he made his way toward the kitchen, only to be intercepted by Lady Munro. "Ah, there ye are." She looked around him to a maid. "Rena, show Kieran to his chamber."

The maid's eyes roved over him and she bit her bottom lip. Kieran wasn't in the mood for a tryst. As a matter of fact, at the moment, his patience was at its limit. "I do not require chambers. I can stay in the stables."

"Nonsense," Lady Munro exclaimed. "I had a room prepared for ye."

Resigned that for the next few days he would not have a moment alone, he followed the maid who swung her hips with so much exaggeration, he wondered if she'd be able to make it up the stairs without stumbling sideways.

Upon arriving at a door, she opened it and motioned inside. "Should ye require anything, all ye have to do is ask."

Kieran's body reacted and he let out a breath. "Perhaps later."

Her smile widened. "I will come to ye tonight."

He nodded and she reached for his arm, allowing her hand to trail down it as she ambled away.

It was a good-sized room, about the same size as his bedchamber at home. Too restless to sit or lay down, he stalked from one side to the other.

Had it been Ethan McLeod who'd attacked Gisela? Why had Ethan sought shelter in her cottage? It made little sense that someone would seek shelter in an enclosed place instead of sleeping outdoors where it is easier to hear others approach.

Then again, the idiot was not of sound mind. It could have been Gisela he was after and something had scared him off. Perhaps her mother's arrival or someone riding near had made Ethan flee.

⇛⇛⇚⇚

THE NEXT MORNING, Kieran woke restless. Even the tryst with the maid the night before hadn't lessened his need to go out and search for Ethan. Leaving his bed just as the sun rose, he was able to head to the stables without anyone seeing him.

Planning a morning ride would perhaps yield some clues as to why Ethan had come through the area.

Laith was anxious to be out. The horse galloped before settling into a slower trot. From where he sat atop his horse, at the side of the slope where the keep was, he had a clear view of the village and the forest.

In the distance, a woman raced away and headed directly toward the forest.

Squinting, he tried to make out the figure, but she was too far. It looked like Gisela, but he didn't know for sure.

"If that woman has gone against her family's wishes, she deserves what she gets." The horse turned his head as if listening. "Ethan could have returned to seek shelter in her cottage," Kieran mumbled.

Laith's ears twitched when Kieran redirected the direction of their travel.

At considering that perhaps Ethan was hiding nearby, the hair on the back of his neck stood up. In the shorter distance now, the woman reached the trees and soon disappeared into the thick foliage.

"Ethan, would ye make it that simple for me?" Kieran guided Laith toward the woods. "I certainly would hope so."

Within moments, he caught up with Gisela, who began to run. Obviously frightened that someone on horseback was chasing her, she didn't slow even when Kieran called out who he was.

Once she arrived at her cottage, she dashed inside, the door slamming behind her.

"Gisela, it's me, Kieran."

There was silence and then a curtain moved and she peered out at him. If he were prone to expressions, he would have probably smiled. There was a smear across her cheek and her hair was disheveled and loose. The dark curls framed her face and fell past her shoulders, a tumble of tangles.

"Ye look like a pauper," he informed her. "Why did ye leave the keep?"

Eyes narrowed, she moved from the window. As he dismounted, she opened the front door. For a moment, they looked to each other in silence. Letting out an exasperated sigh, she moved back and motion for him to come inside.

Kieran entered the tiny but neat cottage.

She lowered to a stool and blew out a breath. "I needed some time alone."

"There are too many people and so much activity at the keep. I am used to a quiet life. When I go to the market, it is only every few days and that is about as much as I can take." The look of dejection was replaced with annoyance as she motioned to him, swinging her right arm. "And yet here ye are."

Kieran gave her a droll look. "I came to ensure ye were safe and that the madman I seek was not about."

"My brave protector." Gisela's tone was flat as she studied Kieran. It astounded him that since meeting him, she'd not once gawked or attempted any kind of flirtation. When her mother had asked if he sought marriage, she'd quickly made up an excuse for him.

"Have ye seen the man who came here and attacked ye since that day?"

Gisela shook her head. "No. I have been with mother since then." She stood and motioned to the door. "Now, if ye would please go, I plan to spend a few hours alone."

"Are ye not worried he could return?"

"I am hoping he forgot how to find me."

Kieran walked outside and around the small cottage looking on the ground and through the trees. In the distance, just a hundred yards or so, a clear river filled with recent rain rushed by.

The sound of the rapid waters and the smell of freshness wafted in the air. Even though the forest trees cast shadows onto the small clearing, it wasn't overly dark. Just enough sunlight trickled through the branches giving the surroundings a magical air.

Gisela walked out and peered up at him. "What are ye looking for?"

"The man that came that day and attacked ye. He could be the one I seek to kill."

Her eyes widened and she took a step backward. "Ye plan to kill someone?"

Kieran studied the ground. "Did he threaten to return?"

Movement in her throat as she swallowed took Kieran's attention. "I do not recall, but I think he did. He probably said it to frighten me. I do not believe he will."

Ensuring to meet her gaze, he shook his head. "I would not be so sure. Ethan McLeod usually does what he says."

Her hand flattened on her chest and once again she swallowed. "Ye are trying to frighten me."

"It does not matter to me if ye are or not," he said and went to Laith. He patted the horse's nose in thought. The woman was willful and would do whatever she wanted. "Ensure ye bolt yer door."

As he rode away, Kieran couldn't help but look over his shoulder. The door to the cottage was closed. The stubborn woman would be her own undoing.

He rode for several hours, keeping an eye out for any trace or sign that Ethan had been there lately.

The pounding of horses' hooves vibrated the ground. A group of men rode toward him and, immediately, Kieran recognized his clan colors. The archers had arrived, which meant his mother and sister would soon follow.

"Ye left without telling anyone." As soon as he came close enough, the head archer Naill, who he'd never quite gotten along with, glared at him. "We lost valuable time searching for ye before yer brother finally let us depart. He was most cross."

Kieran didn't bother replying. It mattered little to him whether anyone was angry with him. His brothers, more than anyone, should understand his desire to act.

Their guards who'd been patrolling the lands had been attacked and one had died. The fatally injured man had managed to tell them it was Ethan who'd set a trap and attacked.

Just like his father, the men hadn't had a chance to defend themselves as he'd attacked them without provocation. Why were his brothers or clan members not as enraged? For him, the need for revenge was renewed, fueled to a level of wanting to see the man responsible for his father's death killed.

"When do the others arrive?" he asked in a bored tone.

"Mid-morning tomorrow." Naill motioned for the other archers to go forth. One, a younger man too naïve to notice the animosity between the men, rode up to Kieran. "I hear ye beat the Munro's son at the last games."

Kieran nodded. "They are preparing for a tournament now. He will compete again."

The young man's grin stretched wide. "I hope to be allowed to as well." He gave him an expectant look. Kieran shrugged. "Ye can if ye wish."

"He is not ready to represent our clan," Naill said, coming alongside. "I will choose the team." There was a challenge in the man's stare. "Tis my duty."

The man was right, but as the late laird's son and now brother to the new laird, Kieran could order Naill to do his bidding. He never would. Mainly because, although Naill and he didn't see eye-to-eye, Kieran wasn't interested enough to care about trivial things like a tournament. He'd given up being the leader of the archers since his father's death and the burden now fell on Naill.

Upon returning to Munro Keep, Kieran searched out the laird to inform him the archers had arrived. Caylen stood just inside the entry with another guard and stopped speaking at noticing his entrance.

"Ye must feel confident by yer absence at the practice yesterday." The smug man looked him up and down.

"I practiced," Kieran replied, but did not elaborate. "I seek yer father."

Caylen's eyes narrowed and he motioned to the stairwell. "He will come down shortly."

"I will request lodging for the archers who've arrived just now."

At this, Caylen straightened, taking notice. "I do not understand how yer clan's style of travel works. Shouldn't the archers remain out to ensure yer sister's party is safe?"

If not for decorum, Kieran would walk away from the man. The soft insult did not annoy him as much as the idiot's pure presence did. "What is to say some are not?"

Just then, Gisela's mother hurried down the stairs and straight to them. Her eyes wide, she stopped and looked from Caylen to him. "Have ye seen my daughter? She is gone."

"Gone?" Caylen took the woman's hand. "I am sure she is about. I will help ye search her out."

The woman's cheeks reddened at the attention and she batted her eyelashes. Kieran fought not to groan out loud.

"That would be lovely, but I am certain that she went out to that dreadful cabin of hers in the forest." Mrs. Munro then looked to Kieran. "Perhaps ye could go see about her? Would ye be a dear and send someone to fetch her?"

"Nay," Caylen said a bit too loudly. "I will see about the mischievous lass." His lips curved as he met Kieran's gaze. "Kieran is much too busy with his clan matters."

"Oh," the flustered woman said. "I beg yer pardon, I did not mean to imply ye had time to spare."

Kieran slid a look to Caylen. The man seemed anxious to go and he had an idea why. Gisela was alone.

"I saw her this morning. She headed to the village," he lied. "I was out for a ride. She assured me that she'd return later today."

Mrs. Munro brightened. "I feel silly. I forget her affinity for herbs that she loves to acquire for her concoctions."

"I will fetch her nonetheless," Caylen insisted, a slight curve to his lips. "A lass so lovely should not be out and about alone."

"Ye are kind," the woman said, tugging him toward the door.

As much as Kieran doubted Caylen's true intentions, he needn't worry about the willful lass. He'd already tried to talk her out of remaining in her cottage. At the same time, the idea of Caylen alone with her didn't sit well. The man was not above attempting to seduce Gisela. Whether cousins or not, Kieran was sure he would take full advantage if he found her alone.

Hopefully, Caylen had believed him when saying she'd gone to the village.

Letting out a breath at spotting Laird Munro, Kieran approached. "Laird, my archers have arrived. Would ye like to see them?"

It was customary for the host laird to meet all people who came and Laird Munro nodded. "Aye, of course. Let us go with haste. I would like to welcome yer men and then see about a meal. I find myself quite hungry."

They went to the courtyard where his archers stood in two rows of five. Except for Naill, who was built like a warrior, the men were almost identical in size and build. Slender, but with bodies honed from hours of horseback riding and archery. Their proud stances and hard expressions were impressive and it was clear the laird found it to be so.

"Welcome men. My staff will see to yer accommodations and the stable master will ensure yer horses are fed and watered. Ye are welcome to come into the great room to break yer fast and also for last meal tonight."

Laird Munro looked to Kieran. "When does yer family arrive?"

"Tomorrow late morning."

"Very well. I will ensure Lady Munro is informed."

Kieran walked with the archers in search of the stable master.

It was a rash decision, but he found Laith, saddled him and headed back out the front gates toward the forest.

CHAPTER FOUR

GISELA FINISHED SWEEPING the cottage and sat down at the table. As much as she wished to remain there, it was best to return to the keep and see about what was happening. It had been childish to slip away and come there, but a part of her wanted to deny what would soon happen.

Once she married, it was probable that she would never return to her cottage, to the home where she found peace. Although small, the cottage provided everything she needed. It smelled of herbs and flowers from her soap making and light filtered in just right both at sunrise and sunset.

Letting out a long sigh, she was about to stand when the sound of a horse approaching made her hesitate. If someone peered in the windows, she'd be visible where she was, so she darted up and hid by standing against a corner.

There were two loud knocks. "Gisela, are ye there? Yer mother requested I come for ye." It was her cousin, Caylen.

Gisela narrowed her eyes. Caylen's voice grated on her nerves. The man had always been overly flirtatious and never hesitated to touch her.

"Gisela!" he called out louder.

When she returned to the keep, it would certainly not be

with Caylen. The man made her uncomfortable. Gisela pressed herself tighter into the corner and held her breath.

Finally, a few moments later, the sounds of departure allowed her to take a deep breath. She hurried to where she'd prepared a bundle of items to take back to the keep with her and then doused a candle on the small table where she'd been sitting earlier. Once enough time had passed that Caylen wouldn't see her, she'd hurry back to the keep.

If only she'd been able to get her horse, it wouldn't take so long to get back and she'd not be exposed as much. However, fetching the animal from the stables would have roused suspicion.

Minutes later, as she reached the front door, a noise outside startled her. Had she been wrong in assuming Caylen had left? She looked to the window and gasped at hazel eyes meeting hers.

Kieran.

What was he doing there? Had he and Caylen run in to each other?

"What do ye want?" Gisela snapped. This man, she wished to avoid for entirely different reasons. It took a great amount of willpower not to touch him, push the locks away from his brow, or run a hand down his arm.

Kieran had an effect on her, one that brought out not just the wanton in her, but also the need to stay in his presence. Just the night before, she'd dreamed of him kissing her. It had been wonderful and also horrible, because she shouldn't have such thoughts of the man.

She went to the front door, removed the latch and opened it. "I require ye to leave. I do not feel like company at the moment."

"Is that why Caylen returned to the keep alone?" He lifted a brow, making him look even more devilishly handsome.

Gisela hitched her chin. "I did not speak to him."

"I should consider myself privileged then?"

Why had she said that? "I plan to return to the keep today, but will do so when I wish, not when it is demanded of me."

He studied her for a long moment, making her wonder what

he was thinking. "What will happen when ye marry? Yer husband will have the last say in what ye do."

The statement was true, causing her shoulders to fall. "I do not know." Gisela met his gaze. "Do ye think it fair that a woman must be dominated entirely by her husband?"

"A man must protect and ensure the best for his wife."

"But is it fair?"

When he let out a sigh and looked up to the sky, Gisela expected he'd not reply with a good answer. But then he surprised her. "Nay, tis not fair. I would hate for yer spirit to be crushed. I hope the man ye marry will see the value in yer independence."

Gisela blinked. Without thought, she threw her arms around his neck, pulled him down and planted a hard kiss on his parted lips.

"Thank ye for saying that," she exclaimed. Then not stopping to ponder her actions, because it would make her head spin, that she'd had the gall to do such a thing, Gisela swung away. "I will fetch my satchel and return to the keep with ye then." She kept her tone light.

Bag slung across her body, she hurried around him to the waiting silver-hued horse. It was best to ignore what she'd just done because if she thought about it, she'd have to admit how strongly she wished for more.

Kieran neared, his hands circling her waist, gaze on hers. Without expression, he lifted her to the horse and then mounted. He urged his mount to a fast pace, his body rigid behind hers.

"Do not ever do that again," he spoke into her ear in a harsh, tense tone.

Gisela attempted to turn and look at him, but he pulled her against his chest. It was impossible to do more than sit straight and keep her eyes forward. It also proved as useless to ignore the hardness of his chest against her back. Gisela took shallow breaths the entire time, praying that they'd arrive so she could flee from him.

What had possessed her to kiss him? His reaction, the statement had to be the most humiliating thing that had ever happened to her. Now, as she fought tears of regret, Gisela became angrier.

"I should have gone with Caylen," she said in an attempt to annoy Kieran. "He would not force me to sit so uncomfortably."

Kieran didn't reply, but loosened his hold and she leaned as far forward as possible.

The keep came into view. Along with it, there were several cartloads of people arriving. No doubt, they traveled for the festivities to take place. Eldest son to the laird, Patrick Munro, was to marry Laird Ross' only daughter, which meant much fanfare.

From what she'd overheard, there would be music, feasting and competitions between both clans' archers and guards. If Kieran competed, she would most definitely not cheer for him.

Suddenly, the horse stopped. Kieran dismounted and pulled her not-so-gently from the horse.

"Wh-what are ye doing?" Gisela stared up at him, her heart pounding. The sack she held slipped from her grasp and hit the ground with a loud cracking sound. Although she'd ensured to wrap her favorite cup carefully with several cloths, now it was broken.

"Ye broke my cup!" She tried to smack his arm, but he caught her wrist.

He stared down at her for a long moment until her eyes widened. Something flickered across his face. At first, he scowled, then his nostrils flared. Finally, his jaw clenched and Kieran visibly swallowed.

Perhaps he was attempting to keep his temper in check. But she'd done nothing to make him angry. If anything, it was she who was due an apology at the moment.

"I did not mean to say what I did," he finally stated. "Do not be mistaken, Gisela. The reason I do not wish ye to kiss me is because I have a hard time resisting ye."

His hands cupped her face and, in an instant, his mouth

crashed over hers with the intensity of a roaring fire. Like embers fanned by a strong wind urging them to burst into flames. Intense passion consumed Gisela and she leaned into him, unable to remain standing without support.

The strength of his arms around her was like a shelter from a storm. She reciprocated by circling his waist and, in that moment, her world was perfect. The kiss continued, his mouth traveling over hers, tongue delving past her lips and into her mouth.

It was like nothing she'd ever experience, so very personal. Gisela had never considered that kissing was such an intimate experience of tasting, nipping and suckling. A learning of what affected the other and intensifying the longer it went.

A low growl, or maybe a moan erupted from deep within his chest as he pulled her closer, his hands sliding up her back, cupping the back of her head as he tilted her so that he could continue to kiss her. Kieran trailed his lips from her mouth to her throat.

As if standing close to a fire, heat rushed from every extremity to pool in the center of her body.

Gisela raked her fingers through his hair, enjoying the feel of the silken tresses against her hands. Needing to touch more of him, she slid her hand down his back. His body was so strong, hard, sheltering her from the whirlwinds that brewed around them. He tasted so good, his lips warm and supple against hers. When his hands traveled down her body to pull her harder against him, a sound erupted from deep in her throat.

"Mmmm." The sound she made was like a hum, but it was loud enough that it penetrated and then the spell was broken.

They jerked apart as if doused with cold water.

Kieran's chest lifted and lowered, his eyes just wide enough that she realized he was as shocked by what had just occurred as she was.

"I…" he started and Gisela held up a hand to quiet him.

"This never happened and it will never happen again." She cursed her breathlessness and inability to keep from gulping for air as she yanked her satchel from the ground, the pottery clanking inside, and she raced toward the keep. Although she knew he would not follow and try to stop her, Gisela had to get away.

Why had he done that? Why had she wanted more?

It was the worst mistake to give a man like Kieran any rights over her body. He would never be for her and she preferred it so. Because a man like him was like flowing water; one could hold it in a vessel but, slowly over time, it disappeared.

Cheeks flushed and breathing hard, she crossed the courtyard intent on finding her mother.

"I tried to find ye." Caylen blocked her path into the keep. "Where have ye been?" His eyes narrowed on her mouth and she realized it must be swollen from Kieran's kisses.

She let out a long breath and held up her sack. "I went to fetch some items…" Gisela stopped abruptly as there was no reason to explain herself to Caylen.

"I went to yer cottage," he replied, a slight sneer to his upper lip. "Were ye there with someone?"

"Up until a few moments ago, I was alone." She hoped he'd figure out she intimated to being with a man and would leave her alone. However, her reply had the opposite effect.

"I would like to be alone with ye," Caylen said as he reached for her face, his fingers a bit too rough as he cupped her jaw. "When can it be, sweet one?"

The words made her swallow the bile taste that rose in her throat. "Tis best we do not, *Cousin*," she replied, emphasizing their relationship. For some odd reason, by the way his lips curved, the idea of them being related seemed to arouse him.

Caylen took her by the arm in a strong hold that did not allow her to slip free. "Let us go speak alone. Father wishes me to find a wife. Would an announcement of our betrothal not be a welcome addition to the festivities?"

Her stomach curdled and she looked over her shoulder toward the entrance. Perhaps it had been rash of her to spend the day away and not in search of a husband. The idea of marrying Caylen was enough to make her want to run away forever.

Just as they entered the main room, Gisela pulled back, not allowing him to tug her to a darkened hallway. "Mother is looking for me. I need to find her. Will ye help me?"

Caylen loosened his grip enough to allow her to get free. She didn't attempt to move away, fearing he'd become angry and lash out. "I believe she is in the sitting room upstairs at this time."

"It will not take long to speak to my father," He said stubbornly. Then he placed his arm around her shoulder, his fingers digging into her shoulder. When her mother appeared from the direction of the kitchens, Gisela yanked away and hurried to her.

"Where have ye been?" Her mother frowned at Gisela but her features smoothed at noticing Caylen. "Thank ye for finding her."

"He did not…" Gisela began, but he interrupted her.

"I plan to speak to Father about marrying Gisela," Caylen said, his chin lifted in challenge, his hand tightening on her shoulder.

For the first time in a long time, her mother was speechless, her eyes widening just enough. "Ye are cousins?" The words came out like a question.

Caylen waved her mother's sentence aside. "That is not a problem. Cousins marry all the time"

"Yes it is," Gisela gritted out. "I'd rather die than marry ye."

Both her mother and Caylen gave Gisela incredulous looks for speaking so boldly, but she didn't care. Best that he saw whom he'd be tied to. "I will choose the man I marry. Try me on this and I will run away."

Caylen took her by both shoulders in a grip that made her wince. Gisela narrowed her eyes. She would not allow anyone to force her into something she didn't wish to do. Whether it was her mother or the idiot cousin of hers.

"Let me go, ye are hurting me," Gisela said with a grimace, as his fingers digging into her skin did indeed hurt. "Release me at once."

Caylen did the opposite and shook her so hard, her head bobbed back and forth. "Ye are not to ever speak to me in that manner."

When he tightened his grip even more, her mother came to her side. "The lass is willful, but no need to mistreat her. I will set her straight."

Taking advantage of the distraction, Gisela kneed him in the groin. When he yelped and released her, she slapped him across the face. "How dare ye," she screamed.

In that instant, the realization of what she'd just done sunk in and she stumbled backwards, aware that unlike when they were children, she could not strike a laird's son. The consequences of her actions could be dire.

"I-I did not mean…" Gisela wanted to curse when her back touched a wall. The only escape would be to run back through the great room. But for that, she'd have to get past a red-faced, groaning Caylen.

His face contorted, nostrils flared and lips curled. The man was furious and he was about to take out every single ounce of it on Gisela.

"What have ye done?" her mother whispered. "Oh, Gisela."

Refusing to back down, Gisela met Caylen's gaze. "I should not have hit ye, but ye should not have hurt me."

"This will not end well for ye," Caylen replied, his face twisted in pain and anger. "I do not wish a shrew like ye for a wife. However, ye will be punished for this."

He motioned a guard over. "Take her to my father's study immediately."

The guard didn't touch her. Instead, he motioned to a corridor on the opposite side of the room.

Caylen turned on his heel and hurried ahead of them.

"This is not good," her mother walked alongside stating the obvious. "Not good at all."

Just then, Lady Munro called out. "Where are ye going?" She

had appeared from a side corridor and caught up to them. Her curious gaze moved from Gisela to the guard. "What is happening?"

"She struck yer son Lady Munro," the guard replied, giving Gisela a light push at the center of her back. "We go to speak to the laird now."

Lady Munro's eyebrows rose. "What did he do?"

"Who?" Gisela, her mother and the guard asked at once.

"Caylen, of course," Lady Munro said.

"He was most cruel with her," her mother replied, dabbing at invisible tears. "Her shoulders and arms will be bruised horribly."

Lady Munro looked to Gisela in question.

She let out a long breath. "He became angry when I told him we cannot marry because we are cousins. When I lifted my voice to ensure he listened, he took me by the shoulders and shook me."

Gisela suppressed the flicker of hope in her chest.

If by some miracle Lady Munro took her side over Caylen's, nothing would happen to her. "Then he squeezed my shoulders until I was to the point of crying, so I kicked him."

"This is ridiculous. We do not have time for petty grievances between cousins. My eldest is about to marry." Lady Munro lifted her skirts. "Come along, we will make this right."

The four of them, including the guard walked into the laird's office where Caylen stood drinking from a cup, a petulant look on his face. Gisela winced upon seeing the red mark from the slap across his left cheek.

"Husband, we do not have time for squabbles between these two. There are much more important matters to take yer attention," Lady Munro began.

"Did ye know Caylen asked to marry Gisela?" the laird asked, not seeming at all put off by the idea.

"I do not wish to marry her any longer," Caylen said. "She is a wildling without proper manners."

Lady Munro looked to her son. "If ye wish to marry, then

court the girl, although I must point out that she is quite put off with ye at the moment. Ye are family, so that may bring some consideration."

Crossing the room, Lady Munro fixed her son with a direct look. "Ye will not do anything to distract from the marriage ceremony. Do ye hear me? We shall wait to speak of this until after the wedding."

Gisela wanted to scream that she'd prefer death to marrying the idiot.

Immediately, memories of Kieran's kiss resurface and she pushed them away. Men only caused problems.

"I need fresh air," Gisela turned and left the study, her mother walking alongside.

"Ye are fortunate the Munro is family. Otherwise, the consequences of what ye did could have been horrible." Just then, her mother leaned forward and studied her face. "What happened to yer lips?"

CHAPTER FIVE

GUIDING A HORSE with one arm had become second nature to Ian McElroy. As head guard for Ross Clan, he was proud of himself and the progress he'd made since the battle in which he'd been left with life-threatening injuries that included the loss of most of his left arm.

At the moment, Ian sat atop his horse, his gaze directly on the horizon. It was a clear day and he could see for quite a distance. There were tall trees on one side and on the opposite side were open fields, plush with green vegetation and flowers. The last portion of the travel should be without trouble as it would be impossible for anyone to approach without being seen.

In the last few months, he'd traveled constantly, rarely spending more than a few days at Ross Keep where he lived. Every day since a bloody battle in which he was left for dead, he was thankful to have survived and even more so for being allowed to remain as guard.

Ian was part of the entourage escorting Lady Ross and her daughter to the wedding at Munro Keep. While he waited for the rest of the guards to mount so they could set off for their second day of travel to Munro lands, a restlessness returned.

Having lost his left arm just above the elbow, he handled the reins with his right hand and guided the horse to the carriage where Lady Ross and her daughter, Verity, were.

"Are ye prepared, ladies?" he asked, not looking in. Both women had complained nonstop since the beginning of the trip and he preferred not to see pointed looks to his severed arm.

"Would ye be able to defend us at all?" Verity Ross had asked the day before.

Her mother had shaken her head, adding, "Sometimes I wonder at Malcolm's decision to keep ye on as guard."

He'd ignored them and now that they'd be gone to live elsewhere, he wasn't unhappy to see them go.

"No, we are not prepared to travel more, but what choice do we have?" Verity replied to his question. "This is the most uncomfortable choice of routes."

Tristan came up beside him and gave him a resigned look. "Mother, Sister, we will arrive by midday if we leave now."

The women didn't respond and Ian followed Tristan to the front. "I will ride a bit ahead. We are traveling along McLeod lands."

Tristan nodded. "Aye, not too far from where we were attacked when returning from Mackenzie lands."

As the day progressed, Ian rode in front of the party with another guard. Time passed slowly, but it was pleasant enough.

As they neared Munro Keep, his thoughts went back to Ross Keep and he wondered how long they'd remain away this time.

Although he treasured his position as guard, he was anxious to spend more time at the place he considered home.

For months now, he'd kept his distance from Ceilidh, a beautiful lass, who was companion to his laird's wife. However, he missed catching glimpses of her. With blonde hair and a lithe body, the lass was beautiful. Often, he'd replayed the one time they'd been together.

She'd caught him just outside the keep courtyard at the woods' edge. They'd kissed for a long time and she'd felt so good against him. It had been madness how far they'd gone, almost to the point of actual lovemaking.

Thankfully, Ceilidh had been the more reasonable of the two and stopped them from going further. They'd lingered on the forest ground for a long time, lying next to each other, holding hands, fingers interlaced.

His lips curved at the romantic notion of collecting a small river stone from where they'd lain.

Since that day, each time he saw her, it took Herculean effort to keep from speaking to her and renewing their friendship. However, he knew she wished for more from him and Ceilidh was not the type of woman a man toyed with.

She was not only beautiful, but also passionate and caring. She'd been the one who nursed him back to health, had been there through his entire recovery.

How could he repay her by tying her to him for life? He was without an arm and was probably kept on as guard only out of pity.

"Ian?" Tristan came up and gave him a quizzical look. "I have been calling to ye." His friend's lips curved. "Is yer head up in the clouds?"

Heat rushed to his face, a telltale sign that he was caught. "Thinking of our route ahead," he lied.

"Ah, well," Tristan said, looking around. "Ye just rode away from the rest of the party."

Ian looked about and as Tristan had stated, he was indeed off the path and heading into the trees. "I have to relieve myself."

It was obvious Tristan didn't believe him, but the man nodded. "Aye, well, catch up when ye're done." He rode off back to where the rest of the party continued ahead.

"Stupid," Ian muttered, dismounting and going into the woods. Moments later, he emerged from behind some bushes and went to his horse. The warmth of the sun heated his back and it felt good. Summer would soon approach and he looked forward to the warmer days.

Would Ceilidh and Malcolm's wife continue their daily walks

to the flower field? He often watched from atop the guard tower enjoying the view of a carefree Ceilidh, hair blowing in the breeze and…

"Ian!" a guard called, riding up. "Ye coming?"

"Aye." Ian grabbed his horse's reins. "Stop being an idiot," he muttered to himself.

"What?" the guard asked. "I cannot hear ye."

"I said, let's catch up."

Ross Keep

WALKING THROUGH THE great room to see what duties needed attending to, Ceilidh pondered at how much her life had changed.

She was more than happy to help Elspeth, her best friend, with the duties of running the household. Since her friend's marriage to Laird Malcolm Ross, Ceilidh's life had improved significantly and she was thankful for each second.

Once, she'd lived in a humble cottage with her family in Kildonan, a small village on nearby lands. Now, her beautiful chamber was almost as big as the entire humble home was.

Servants saw to most of her needs even though she considered herself a servant of sorts. Elspeth refused to see her as such, instead naming her a companion.

Ceilidh cared little what she was called and spent her days helping wherever she was needed even doing the most menial of duties. She was happy. Her family was nearby. Her closest friend and she lived together. And best of all, Elspeth was happy.

A maid approached, linens piled high in her arms. The young woman gave her a wry smile. "Time to change the smelly guards' beds."

Ceilidh followed her as she walked toward the corridor where the guards' rooms were. There were only four rooms. Two for men Ceilidh didn't know well, one was Naill's and the other Ian's.

She caught up with the servant. "I will do two and ye the other two." She grabbed linens from the top of the pile and hurried down to the last two doors.

Once inside the first room, she left the door open and hurried about to ensure the work was done quickly. She'd promised Elspeth to go with her to the flower field so it was best not to dally about.

It took only a few moments to freshen the bed and sweep out the room. Then she went to the last room. It was Ian's room and she hesitated at the doorway. She considered asking the girl to switch with her, but felt silly. The fact that Ian had ignored her since recovering from his devastating injuries was something she had to get used to. It was for the best that if a man didn't desire a woman, the woman should turn her attention elsewhere.

From what she had observed, a man liked to chase after a women and after having his way with her, act as if nothing ever happened, often leaving the lass confused and lovesick.

She would not act like that and if he wished to add her to his conquest list, then so be it. As a matter of fact, she had made up her mind to speak to Ian and inform him there was no reason for him to continue avoiding her. She'd tell him they would leave the past behind them and move forward with their lives.

Separately, of course.

Thinking back to the many times she'd cried over being ignored by Ian, Ceilidh became annoyed. She hurried into his room and yanked back the sheets. She opened the window to allow fresh air in and upon throwing the dirty sheets into the hallway, she began to sweep.

The room was clean, but it smelled like him. Woods and fresh air, yes, that is what he'd smelled of when they'd spent time together. In the woods beside the keep, they'd kissed and held hands. She huffed and swept with vigor although there wasn't much in the way of dirt on the floor.

She spread the clean linens on the bed and huffed in annoyance. "Nothing to do in this room and definitely no reason to meander about like a homesick child."

Next to the bed was a small table, upon it a lantern and a small rock. Interesting what some people collected.

After one last look about the room, she left.

CHAPTER SIX

"THEY ARRIVE," A guard from atop the gates at Munro Keep called out and a group of people gathered in the courtyard to look toward the gates.

Kieran went to stand just behind the laird's family at the front entrance to the home.

"Yer family arrives with much fanfare," a woman said, tapping his arm. It was someone he did not recognize. He nodded and returned his attention to the proceedings. After a few moments, the woman moved away.

The Munro family flanked the laird, as was the custom. Caylen stood next to a less than happy looking Gisela. If the man meant to marry the lass then Kieran pitied him more than her. She was strong and independent and would not allow the shallow idiot to take advantage of her. At least, that is what he hoped.

However, women had little power in a marriage. It would be a shame for her spirit to be broken.

His brother, Tristan, and guard, Ian, led the Clan Ross party followed by another two guards, the carriage, a cart with trunks and, lastly, ten guardsmen and six archers.

They rode through the gates and the carriage came to a stop at the bottom of the steps leading to the main house.

Two Ross guards dismounted and opened the carriage doors. His mother emerged, secondly his sister, followed by their companions.

Laird Munro, Lady Munro and Patrick, who would marry his sister, went down the steps to extend a warm welcome.

Kieran let out a breath and stepped back until his back was almost at the wall. Out of the corners of his eyes, he caught sight of Gisela slipping away around the side of the house.

In a couple of seconds, he was sure Caylen would follow. But as his brother, Tristan, approached to greet the laird and the party made their way into the keep, Caylen remained with the group.

Once he greeted his mother and sister, he did not follow them inside and instead walked to the side of the house to see what Gisela was doing.

At first, he didn't see her. But after a few moments, he spotted her sitting on a bench, head bent as if in prayer.

She rubbed her shoulder and gingerly lowered the top of her blouse to peer at it. A dark, angry bruise purpled the otherwise fair skin. She touched it and winced.

"What happened?"

At his question, she jumped, her eyes jerking up to his. She pulled up the blouse, covering the bruise. "I ran into a…wall."

"No, ye did not," he replied, staring into her eyes. "The truth."

Gisela huffed. "I do not know why ye care enough to ask." When she sighed, Kieran considered if perhaps his assertion of her ability to not be broken was wrong.

In a faraway voice, she spoke. "Perhaps I shall escape and go to live with my mother's family. My aunt and uncle live in a beautiful tiny fishing village by the sea."

Although he shouldn't particularly care, Kieran couldn't stop his curiosity when it came to Gisela. She piqued his interest like no one ever had before. "Who hurt ye?"

"I resisted a man's advances. He did not take well to rejection." Gisela shrugged. "I can defend myself."

His gut clenched, fury rising. Anyone who hurt people less strong, unable to defend themselves, was without honor. "Who?" he asked through clenched teeth. "Tell me, Gisela."

With raised eyebrows and wide eyes, she looked up at him. "Ye have never said my name before." She stood. "Ye know who. But it matters not. I have put him in his place."

Kieran took a step toward her. Her blouse slipped down off her left shoulder. The top of the bruise was visible and he found it impossible to look away. He reached toward her, but pulled back. "Stay away from him." Kieran turned on his heel and walked away.

HAD HE MEANT to reach for her and attempt to kiss her again? Gisela considered that as Kieran disappeared around the corner toward the entrance to the home. Why would he care what happened to her?

If she were to be honest, her head spun from the strange actions of men. Caylen was a horrible person who used his position as the laird's son to full advantage and acted like a tyrant. He'd claimed that he'd have her and her family thrown from Munro lands if she didn't come to his bed. Idiot. Her father had seen that they were well taken care of and without need from the laird. Besides, her uncle and aunt would never agree to it.

She could not tell her brother what Caylen had done. Hamus was proud of his work at the stables, however, he would not hesitate to beat their cousin to a bloody pulp and then take her and her mother away if he saw the bruise.

Laird Munro would not toss them off the lands on the word of his weak, idiot son. Unless it was a grave incident, they were safe. Perhaps she could speak to Lady Munro.

Her mother appeared. She looked around and upon spotting her, hurried toward Gisela.

"Lass, what are ye doing out here? Lady Munro requires our help. The wedding party is here." Her mother's wide smile faltered at seeing her bruised shoulder and Gisela yanked the blouse up and tied the strings.

"He hurt ye."

"What that idiot does is annoy me. Hopefully, Caylen will hold true to the fact he no longer wishes to marry me. I cannot say I can keep from slapping him again if he insists on it."

"Ye should have a cup of honey mead to help with the pain," her mother said distractedly, her gaze moving toward the courtyard and the front of the house.

"I will come with ye. Pray that I do not see my cousin and feel a need to strike him again."

Her mother's expression became hard, which was alarming. "I will not give him the satisfaction of ye getting punished. I have a plan in mind to make him pay for mistreating ye." Before Gisela could stop her, her mother raced away, arms pumping, and a murderous expression on her face.

"Oh, no." Gisela returned to the bench. "What now?"

Letting out a breath, she hurried to the entrance by the kitchens. Upon entering through the doorway, she was greeted by a chaotic scene. Maids hurried to and fro, some with spoons in hands, others with trays filled heavy with bowls of food. Most of them ignored Gisela as she went into the room hoping to find her mother who often went to the kitchens when upset.

"What do ye wish for, lass?" the red-faced cook asked.

"My mother?"

"Not here."

The entire situation was getting more annoying by the moment. If only there was a way to convince her mother to leave the keep.

Gisela hurried down a corridor until arriving at the great room. Almost every seat was filled. People sat drinking ale and mead. Some had bread in hand. There were only a few from Clan Ross. Most of those in attendance were Munros.

At the head table were the laird and his eldest son.

A scan of the room was enough to know Caylen was not about. Lady Munro, Lady Ross and her daughter were not in the room either. And neither was her mother.

She hurried across the room to the stairwell. Although she and her mother shared a room on the main floor, she figured her mother had followed the wedding party upstairs.

Once she arrived at the larger chambers, the sounds of women's voices became loud.

She stopped at the doorway of a room and peeked in. Lady Munro and Lady Ross sat with Kieran's sister. They spoke animatedly, while several other women listened adding a comment here and there. It seemed they were planning the proceedings that would take place the next day.

Her mother was not in the room, which made Gisela begin to panic. If her mother did something rash, the consequences could be dire.

"What are ye doing snooping about?" Caylen stood next to her, his expression as if he smelled something horrible.

"I am looking for my mother."

He sniffed. "Why would someone of yer family's standing be in the same room as these ladies?"

Gisela fought the urge to shove past him. "Not only is she yer aunt, but we have been asked to assist by yer mother."

"Ye should go search for her in the servants' quarters, or perhaps in a man's bed." He stalked past her.

Glaring at his retreating back, Gisela figured she much preferred a rude Caylen to him pursuing her.

Finally, she found her mother in their chamber. Lillian had a pot over the fire and was sprinkling herbs into it.

"What are ye doing?" Gisela neared and sniffed.

Her mother gave her a knowing look. "Making a bit of tincture, nothing more."

Gisela decided not to ask. Her mother would not follow through and do something to hurt her friendship with Lady

Munro. However, she seemed to be relishing the thought of doing something to Caylen.

"Please do not do something rash. Once this wedding is over, we should return back home to the village."

Instead of a reply, her mother began to hum.

AT LAST MEAL, Gisela sat away from her mother who insisted on always sitting at the front of the room. Lillian always took control of every conversation, informing everyone that she was part of the Munro family and therefore entitled.

She knew her mother would be looking for her, but the last thing Gisela wanted at the moment was to be in Caylen's direct sight. Hopefully, his ire would ebb as time progressed and she could return home and all would be in the past.

Last meal that day was festive. Platters piled high with meats and root vegetables were placed on every table. There were not as many people in attendance as the days before, since many had been sent home.

At a table next to the high board was Kieran, who sat with his mother, brother and sister. The women spoke animatedly while the two brothers ate in silence. Every once in a while, Kieran nodded at something said.

It was interesting to note that his expression always remained the same. Whether with his family or speaking to others, the ever-present scowl seemed to indicate he'd rather be anywhere but there.

"What do ye find so interesting?" A young woman lowered to the bench across the table from her. "Tis good eating today." The woman reached for a piece of meat and began eating with gusto.

"Do I know ye?" Gisela asked while studying the woman. She was short and round, with bright red cheeks and curly brown hair. Her eyes were a bright blue and she seemed quite at home there at the keep.

"No, probably not. I am Helen. I am Lady Verity's companion." The young woman grabbed a second piece of meat and piled vegetables onto her plate. "I love celebrations," she exclaimed, bits of food falling from her mouth to land on her bosom.

Helen looked to the head table. "The groom looks less than enthusiastic."

Indeed, Patrick Munro looked down at his plate, not touching it. He didn't particularly look glum, but definitely not happy.

She would describe his expression more as pensive. However, she had to agree with Helen. Given the circumstances, he did not seem in good spirits.

"Have he and yer mistress spent any time together?"

Helen's head bobbed up and down. "Oh, aye, they have. They once walked in the garden. I do believe, another time, they danced."

When she didn't add any more instances, Gisela looked to Verity. The girl's cheeks were flushed. Although quite plain, with a round cherubic face and small eyes, she was an interesting sort. It was curious that Verity did not look to her soon-to-be husband, but seemed more interested in speaking to those at the table.

When Lady Munro neared their table, both Tristan and Kieran stood. Once she sat, they said something and went to the back of the room.

Kieran and his brother took the room's attention. Both were formidable in size and attractive. It went without saying that no one could compare to Kieran when it came to his handsome looks, but Tristan was also very attractive.

When she sighed, Helen looked from her to the brothers.

"Oh. Ye pine for one of them?" the young woman said and smiled widely. "They are very handsome. I am going to miss catching glimpses of the youngest brother on occasion. Although I would never dare approach him." She gave an exaggerated shudder.

"Why do ye react that way?" Gisela whispered.

The young woman leaned forward and spoke in a low tone. "He is quite terrifying. Rarely speaks. Well, except to Moira, who coddles him. She has since he was but a wee babe."

"Who is Moira?"

"The cook. The woman in charge of the kitchens."

Kieran and his brother now sat with some of the Clan Ross guards. They spoke and it seemed Kieran was explaining something to his brother. The other guards at the table listened intently.

"He does not seem a bad sort to me," Gisela said. For some reason, she did not like that the woman thought badly of Kieran. "He is not particularly friendly, but I would not call him terrifying."

"Is that so?" Helen turned to look at Kieran.

In that moment, his gaze lifted and he looked at Gisela. When their gazes met, heat traveled down from her chest to her stomach.

His narrowed gaze moved to Helen and the woman gasped.

Helen shook her head. "Ye are wrong. He is not a nice person at all."

CHAPTER SEVEN

WHEN THE ARROW hit just right of the center, Kieran scowled at the target.

"What are ye going to do, scare it so it will move over?" Tristan said with a chuckle. "Ye have not been practicing at all if I can beat ye."

His brother was right and Kieran wasn't sure if he'd beat Caylen with the way he was missing almost every time.

A group of women had gathered, doing a horrible job of pretending not to watch him. He glanced in their direction, but didn't see Gisela. She wasn't the type to waste time on such things as flirting. His lips twitched at the thought.

"They want us over at the competition area," Naill said, his gaze moving from Kieran to the target. The man had the gall to smile before looking away.

Kieran walked to the target and yanked his arrows from it before going to a large field outside the keep gates where the competition targets were placed.

Despite the fact he would rather be hunting down Ethan McLeod, Kieran looked forward to competition. However, this was to be the first time he'd participated in such a trivial thing since his father's murder and it felt wrong.

He'd enjoyed the day and hadn't felt particularly badly for it. However, in Kieran's opinion, it wasn't the proper time for his family to indulge in recreation.

Men gathered in groups. They were divided in teams of four. He and Tristan along with Naill and another Ross archer were a team.

Caylen pranced about like a damned bird, holding up his bow as if it were a trophy. His team included his brother and two other men who he assumed were part of the Munro's archer guard.

There were another three teams. Mackenzie, Munro and Ross archers would be competing.

Kieran took pride in knowing his men were well skilled and would do well in the competition.

A horn blew and Laird Munro spoke about something or other. Kieran didn't bother to listen, but instead looked to the people seated on the platform. His mother and sister smiled widely and clapped with glee. His heart lightened at the sight. They deserved happiness.

Living with the Munros would suit them both well.

Next to his mother and sister were Lady Ross and Gisela's mother who, like the rest of the women, waved cloths in the air to encourage their archers.

Gisela sat beside her mother. She held a cloth but did not wave it. When meeting his gaze, she hitched her chin up just a bit and gave him a subtle nod. The message was clear.

Beat Caylen Munro.

Kieran frowned. His eyes moved from Gisela and then to Caylen. His brother's lips curved. "Yer lass is quite a beauty," he said with raised eyebrows.

"She is not my lass," Kieran snapped, not liking the pride he felt at his brother's compliment. In truth, Gisela was a rare beauty. With rich brown wavy hair and olive skin, she was striking. Her almond-shaped eyes that lifted at the corners drew one in and her lips, just a bit too wide and thick, were the most enticing he'd ever known.

"Brother?"

Kieran huffed and looked to Tristan. "What?"

"We begin. Do ye wish to go first?"

He stepped up to the marker and looked to the target. He ignored everything and everyone else. He was not competing against anyone but himself. And Kieran knew he was the best archer there.

When he loosed the arrow, making allowance for the light breeze, he didn't have to watch to know it hit just a hair high. Nonetheless, it was in the center. Not the best, but it would do.

There were exclamations from those gathered and loud whispers as each archer took his turn. Everyone was skilled. However, soon it became apparent who the best were. Both Kieran's team and the other Ross team were neck and neck.

Caylen's curses and disparaging remarks to his team of archers made them miss their targets. He then turned his anger to the other teams, calling them out for cheating and such.

His brother stomped over to where Caylen was and towered over the man who looked about to run. "Keep yer comments about my men to yerself." He kept the tone low so as not to be overheard, but Kieran was able to read his brother's lips.

The man finally nodded and, after staring at the man for a bit too long, Tristan returned.

Kieran met his brother's gaze. "Should we allow one of their teams to win?"

His brother's eyes were flat. "Aye, we have to."

"Gavin and I will go to the other team and send two here. We will lose." Kieran hated to, but it was only a stupid competition.

"No," Naill said, surprising him. "I will go."

"We are not going to stand here and argue about this." Tristan let out an annoyed snort.

Their other team of archers came over and looked to them with curiosity. "We have decided to lose."

"The best teams will win." Laird Munro had neared without

them noticing. "Now, return back to yer places."

Everyone walked back to stand with their original teams and, soon after, the second round began. This time, they were to stand a bit farther from the targets. Kieran squinted at the targets. "Ours are a bit further back."

"I noticed," Tristan said and looked to their other team who also seemed to be saying the same thing. "Both?"

"Aye," Kieran replied with a grin. "Good. I am better from farther away."

When it was his turn, his arrow landed dead center, the second one splitting the first. There was applause and people jumped to their feet as he prepared to shoot the third and final arrow.

Beat Caylen. He could feel Gisela's silent request.

Kieran loosed the arrow and it, too, hit the center. There were exclamations and applause, but he only sought Gisela's approval. She clapped and smiled brightly, her twinkling eyes meeting his. A more beautiful sight he'd never seen.

The Munro team won second place. They'd cheated, but being his team won and the other Ross team was third, the Ross archers didn't care about the standings.

There was much drinking and animation at the picnic after the archery competition. Kieran joined the other archers and watched the warriors compete in the stone throw. This time, the other clan seemed to have an edge. Tristan was strong and would probably do well, but having been in battle, he had not had time for trivial things like practice.

Once the wedding ceremony ended the next day, Kieran planned to leave immediately. Hopefully, the scouts he'd sent out to look for signs of Ethan would produce information.

Just then, a group of men caught his attention. They looked familiar.

He went to where Tristan stood watching the other competitors. "Look there by the last tent. Who are they?"

Tristan studied the group, his body straightening. "McLeods. I believe one of them came to our keep once as a messenger."

"Why are they here now?"

"Perhaps the McLeod sends a message to the Munro."

"Go speak to them. Ye are married to one. Find out where the killer is."

Tristan gave him a droll look. "Am I to walk up and say, 'Where is the bastard Ethan? My brother wishes to know so he can kill him.' Is that it?"

"If ye won't, I will then."

His brother's hand shot out taking his upper arm. "I will do it. Just let me throw the damned stone."

Tristan was a good brother.

Kieran had always admired his brother's even temperament. Tristan was a born diplomat.

Unfortunately, the men didn't have any new information. They'd not seen Ethan in weeks.

CHAPTER EIGHT

Ross Keep

CEILIDH STOOD BY the garden gate keeping her gaze away from the front gates as a group of guards returned from the north. If Ian was with them, she preferred not to know, not right away anyway. It wasn't the place or time to confront him.

Besides, it had been a good day. She'd just returned the day before after a wonderful visit with her family and Elspeth's at their village of Kildonan. There was a celebration in the village and spending time there had been soothing to her soul.

For the first time in weeks, she'd been able to not think about Ian and had not pictured him at night as she'd fallen asleep.

He'd been gone more than present in the last weeks and perhaps it was for the best. It had helped her slowly get used to the idea that nothing would ever happen between them.

"Ceilidh?" Elspeth stood by the kitchen door and gave her a quizzical look. "I have been searching for ye."

"For the last few hours, I have worked here," she said as she motioned to the garden. "Why did ye not look here?"

Elspeth laughed. "I came and looked, but now seeing ye wear a green dress, I must have missed ye."

Her friend from childhood was as close as a sister. When Ceilidh's gaze moved past Elspeth to the gates, Elspeth asked, "Did ye see that guards returned?

"Aye, just now."

"I had not thought any would return until after the marriage feasting ended."

"Perhaps they did not wish to remain. Tis not like they would be invited to partake in it." Ceilidh flinched at realizing she'd just complained about the upper stations that her friend was now part of.

"Do not worry. Tis true." Elspeth waved at a pair of men who walked by. "Make sure to come and join us at last meal," she called out.

Ceilidh couldn't keep from peeking. Neither of the men was Ian.

Her friend gave her a knowing look. "He just headed to the front entrance to report to Malcolm."

It made sense. Despite his injury and having lost his left arm, Ian remained leader of the guard and a very able warrior. From what Ceilidh had heard, in battle, he was without compare.

She returned back into the garden, her stomach jittery. "I am almost finished with my tasks. Do ye require something from me?"

"Aye," Elspeth said, walking behind her. "New gowns have arrived, two for me and one for ye. The seamstress wishes us to try them on."

Every time Elspeth got new dresses made, she ordered one for Ceilidh.

Her wardrobe was growing to the point that she sometimes felt uncomfortable about it. However, she loved each of the beautiful gowns and would be hard-pressed to give any away. Already, she'd donated all but two of her older dresses to village poor.

The two dresses that remained, she wore for chores and gardening or whenever she rode a horse.

"Truly?" Ceilidh couldn't help but smile widely. "The blue one?"

"I believe so," Elspeth replied. "I have not seen them as yet. I decided to come and find ye so we could do so together."

When Elspeth grabbed her hand and tugged her toward the house, Ceilidh did not resist and, together, they raced into the house, through the great room where people were gathered and up the stairs.

By the time they reached Elspeth and Malcolm's chambers, they were breathless. The seamstress looked up and gave them a questioning look. "Is all well Lady Ross?"

Elspeth made a shooing motion with her hands. "Julianne, when we are alone, please call me Elspeth."

The seamstress pulled out a gown. "Lady Ross, here is the first of yer gowns." She pulled a beautiful ivory gown that Elspeth had ordered for a summer festival celebration and both of them let out a gasp.

Ceilidh neared the dress, not daring to touch the fabric with her dirty hands. "It is breathtaking."

"Go and bathe," Elspeth ordered. "Ye cannot try on anything in that state." She looked Ceilidh up and down. "Ye're dirty."

"I can see them. I will not touch."

Elspeth pulled on a cord and, within moments, a maid appeared. "Have a bath drawn for Lady Ceilidh. Do so in the kitchens. She will be down momentarily."

"I do not wish to go back through the great room," she admitted, considering that the last thing she wanted was to run into Ian.

"Go down the back corridor then," Elspeth instructed as the seamstress pulled out a second gown. This one was in muted tones of grey.

Finally, a beautiful blue creation was held up for inspection and Ceilidh wanted to weep with joy. It was so very beautiful.

Both forgot about the bath, too fascinated by the wonderful creation.

It was a few minutes later that, finally, Ceilidh made her way down to the bath.

Moira, the cook, gave her an annoyed glance. Although the woman was rough around the edges, she was kind and one of the few people there at the keep that Ceilidh had grown to care for.

"Ye should not be traipsing about my kitchens with those dirty shoes." She gave Ceilidh a pointed look and motioned to behind a set of screens. "Yer bath is ready. There was perfumed oiled added to the pitcher. Use it to rinse yer hair."

"Thank ye." Ceilidh gave her a toothy smile. "I cannot tell ye how excited I am about this bath. Afterward, I can go try on a new dress."

Despite her eye roll, Moira's lips twitched. "Yer water grows cold."

Minutes later as she sunk into the hot water, Ceilidh sighed with contentment. It never ceased to amaze her how wonderful her and Elspeth's lives were now and how fortunate she was that her friend insisted she join her there at Ross Keep.

She washed slowly despite the fact that she was anxious to return upstairs. She hadn't gone near the gown, preferring to wait until she could touch it. With a cloth, she washed away the garden dirt and then sunk further down so that she could rinse her hair and wash it.

THE KITCHEN WAS surprisingly empty when Ian entered. However, the screens were up and he grinned. His mother must have been alerted to his presence and had a bath ready for him. Admittedly, he would have preferred to eat something first, however, the idea of a warm bath was just as alluring.

He walked around the screens and yanked his tunic up over his head. Once that was done, he pulled his boots off and then pushed his breeches down. Totally bare, he looked to the hearth where a large cloth was hung so it would be warm for when he got out of the water.

Taking one step forward, he froze at hearing a gasp.

From the tub, a pair of eyes and a nose hovered just above the water. Wet hair plastered to her head, she attempted to sink further down.

"Why are ye in my bath?" He had said the first thing that came to mind.

Of anyone else in the keep, it was the one woman he did not wish to see at the moment. Not only that, but he stood before her bare as the day he was born.

When her gaze moved between his legs, his body reacted and his staff twitched. Ian dove for the closest cloth and shielded himself. The small patch of fabric barely provided any coverage.

"This is my bath, not yers," Ceilidh replied, having lifted up just enough for her mouth to come above the water. "Leave now."

"I am not dressed."

Her eyes widened. "Dress at once then."

"I can turn my back and allow ye to finish." Ian wasn't sure why he didn't dress and leave. Probably because a part of him wished to catch a glimpse of the beautiful woman's body.

For a long moment, she was silent, her eyes narrowed until they were but slits. "Ye are not a good man, Ian. Ye are without honor."

"Because I mistook yer bath for mine? My mother always has a bath ready for me when I return."

"Not this time," she quipped. "If ye leave, I will finish with haste. Tis not as if ye wish to be in my presence."

His chest constricted at her words. "Ye saved my life. I can never repay what ye did for me. I hope ye know that."

Her right eyebrow rose. "By ignoring my existence? Is that how ye show yer appreciation?"

"No, I have been sent away…"

"Do not toy with me." In her anger, Ceilidh rose up until the tops of her breasts lifted above the water. "If ye do not wish to speak of what happened between us, tis fine. But do not lie to me."

"It is not what ye think." At the view of her full breasts, his thoughts returned to the time they'd been alone in the forest. She'd been perfect, so soft and pliant under body as they'd kissed each other breathless. It was only the fact he was not fully recovered from his battlefield injuries that had prevented him from taking her as his own. He became fully erect, his sex hardening behind the now much too small cloth.

"Ye have no idea what I think." Her voice rose and she sat up higher when pointing a finger at him.

When his gaze fell to her chest, she gasped and sunk into the water. "I will leave momentarily. If ye wish to stand there like a naked statue, then do so. I do not care what ye do."

"I will cover myself." He looked to the larger cloth. With only one hand, he would have to drop the cloth he held before being able to reach for it. "Will ye look away?"

There was a challenge in her eye. "I have seen every part of yer body."

He met her eyes and set his jaw in an effort to intimidate her. "Not like this." Although tempted to remove the cloth and show her, he kept from it and instead looked down to where he held the cloth.

Ceilidh's eyes widened. "Oh." She swallowed visibly. "Turn around then. I will hurry and promise not to look."

He believed her. It wasn't as if any woman could be attracted to a man who was as lacking as him, regardless of being battle ready and able to hold a sword up in battle. He was scarred and with only one arm, he was sure making love to him would be disgusting to a woman like Ceilidh.

That she'd been willing to kiss that one time was due to how kind she was and probably because she'd felt sorry for him. Since his injury, pitying looks and comments were something he grew to hate.

He heard the trickle of water being poured and then there was sloshing as she climbed from the bath. It was quiet for a few moments and he wondered what she was doing. She mumbled softly and he peeked out of the corners of his eyes toward the hearth.

It was the best decision he'd ever made. She dried quickly, her lithe body with curves in the right places became still when she turned to ensure he wasn't looking. He made sure to look straight ahead. With quick movements, she pulled a chemise over her head, allowing him to take one last look as the peaks of her breasts and soft curves of her hips disappeared under the folds of fabric.

Within moments, she was fully dressed and dashed past him. Just before disappearing on the other side of the screen, she met his gaze.

There was hurt in the beautiful blue-green pools. "I had hoped we would be friends or…" She gave a light shrug. "I suppose it matters little to ye." Her gaze swept over him, hesitating at where he held the cloth.

It could have been that he wished it so, but there seemed to be appreciation in her gaze. Before he could know for sure, she was gone.

"IAN, WHATEVER ARE ye doing there? And without a stitch of clothing?" His mother gave him a disapproving look as she rounded the screen. "Ceilidh was quite upset. She is not that kind of a woman."

All he could do was walk where the larger cloths were and took one. He expertly wrapped it around his waist by holding one edge down with the portion of arm he had left on the left. "I did not know she was here. I thought it was my bath."

"What did ye say to make her cry?"

"She was crying?" he gawked. "Why would she be crying?"

Moira shook her head. "I am saddened that my own son is so daft."

He frowned but did not say more as two lads hurried in to empty the bath.

"Once ye bathe, ye will eat. And perhaps in the next day or

so, I will explain to ye the very obvious."

Ian let out a long breath. "I am hungry."

"Bathe first," his mother ordered and stalked around the screen.

CEILIDH WIPED AWAY the tears and hurried into Elspeth's chambers. Her hair dripped and her clothing was plastered to her still damp body.

Upon Ceilidh entering, Elspeth turned and grinned. "Is this not the most divine creation?" She looked beautiful in the ivory gown.

"Of course it is." Ceilidh attempted to match her friend's excitement. "Did I miss ye trying on the other?"

"Ye did, but I can put it on again for last meal." Elspeth motioned to the hearth. "Hurry, dry yer hair. Once Julianne finishes with this, she can ensure any stitching needed for yers is done. We will both wear new gowns tonight."

Thankfully, Elspeth mistook her bright nose and wet hair to being overly excited about the new gown, so she did not ask any questions. In truth, Ceilidh wanted to avoid last meal.

The picture of Ian's nude body stayed forefront in her mind's eye. He was perfection. Despite scars and a missing arm, it did not diminish one bit the attraction she felt for him. She'd thought herself prepared to see him and confront him, but circumstances had taken a horrible turn and now it was impossible to face him and feign nonchalance.

Had he realized how much his presence had affected her? Although she'd seen his body before while nursing him back to health after he'd been left for dead at a battleground, this had been vastly different.

This time, he exuded health and vigor. He was battle-honed and without a hint of weakness. An indescribable aching had surged as she'd fought to keep from moving closer to Ian and reaching for him. Her fingers itched to trace over the rippling muscles of his chest and stomach.

Ceilidh mused that the incident could be considered humorous, if not for the mortification of being discovered in a bath.

"What are ye thinking of so deeply?" Elspeth asked, peering at her intently. "Are ye unwell?"

Ceilidh jumped on the opportunity to miss last meal. "In truth, I feel ill. My head is spinning." It was the truth. Her head was spinning. She gave Elspeth what she hoped was a hopeful expression. "I need to rest. I will miss last meal. Can we wear our new gowns tomorrow?"

A maid entered and giggled upon seeing Ceilidh. "Moira wishes me to tell ye that Ian did not mean to walk in on ye."

Elspeth's eyes rounded and she whirled to look at her. "What happened?" She yanked Ceilidh to the bench by the bed. "Tell me everything."

"I cannot. It was most mortifying."

Her friend never let her curiosity rest and she looked to the maid. "What did Ian walk in on?"

"The mistress bathing," the maid giggled. "He was completely nude."

Not only Elspeth, but also Julianne, the seamstress, dissolved into fits of laughter. Ceilidh tried her best to remain angry, but her lips began to twitch until she, too, began to laugh.

"It was not at all comical," she insisted, trying her best to look serous. "This is horrible."

"Nonsense," Elspeth said. "Ye could not have planned it better. Now ye will wear the new gown and we will ensure ye look beautiful. And of course, ye will ignore him completely."

"Of course," Julianne added and Ceilidh wondered why the woman was suddenly taking such an interest in her love life.

THE ROOM WENT silent when Lady Ross entered the great room at last meal. Ian looked up to see the appealing woman blushing from the attention. Laird Malcolm Ross stood, pride evident in his stance at seeing the beauty that'd he'd made his wife.

Behind Lady Ross, Ceilidh entered and his eyes rounded. Dressed in a pale blue gown that matched her eyes, she seemed to float into the room, head held high. Although her dress was simpler than that of the laird's wife, it suited her perfectly, molding to every curve like a soft breeze.

Her golden hair had been swept up and into a simple style that enhanced the graceful neck and Ian could only imagine pressing his lips against the soft skin.

Immediately, men began to murmur and Ian did his best to ignore the mumblings.

"Did she not nurse ye to health?" One of the guards nudged him. "How much touching was involved?"

Despite the urge to snap at the man, Ian knew it was best not to show his ire. Guardsmen grew bored during long periods of work and would take advantage of any sign of weakness to goad another constantly.

"I was too damned sick to know. Perhaps she took advantage of me and I am not aware."

The men laughed and he slid a second look to where Ceilidh sat. She kept her gaze lowered, speaking to the other women gathered around her table. Not only did she not look in his direction when her gaze lifted, but she seemed to have forgotten all about their earlier interaction.

CHAPTER NINE

Munro Keep

THE AMOUNT OF chaos over the wedding ceremony was enough to drive Gisela to hide under her bed. Everywhere, maids rushed to and from chambers. Her mother was agitated and frenzied over her dress not fitting quite right and then insisted her hair be taken down and combed again. She hadn't exactly helped with the wedding in any way so far, as had been the excuse for them to remain.

Gisela peered out the window to the courtyard where guards put up long tables for visitors who would not fit inside to join in the wedding feast. Carts piled high with chopped wood were being unloaded for bonfires later in the evening.

"I should go help in the kitchen," Gisela said, still looking out. "I am being of little use in here."

Her mother's wide eyes took her in, scanning from her head to her feet. "Oh, no!"

If there was a spider on her, she would have to throw it out the window. "Where is it?" Gisela looked down to her bodice.

"Ye have not dressed yet. Yer hair is a mess." Her mother looked about to faint. "Why are ye standing there looking like a pauper's pet mouse?

"This dress is more than suitable." Gisela hesitated and touched her hair. "I do need to do something about my hair, I suppose."

When her mother screamed, both she and the maid jumped. "Get her dressed. Do her hair. We need someone else in here to help."

"I will do it," the maid said, seeming relieved to not have to continue to do Lillian's hair.

Gisela gave her an apologetic smile. "Thank ye. A simple braid is fine."

"Absolutely not," her mother called from the doorway. "We are the laird's family and cannot embarrass him." She made a motion with her hands, calling someone to her. "Ye, yes, ye. We need help with my daughter's preparation for the wedding. Fetch a maid or two."

"Mother, really. I have been dressing myself every day. I am already dressed."

"No, ye are not." Her mother rushed to the wardrobe and pulled out a dress. "This is what ye are wearing."

The forest green dress was beautiful, but the bodice would be much too revealing since it was obviously made for someone with a much smaller bust.

"Where did ye get that?" Gisela shirked away when her mother neared with it. "It is not mine."

"I asked Lady Munro for a dress for ye and she was gracious enough to find it. It was left behind by a very wealthy widow."

Once she put the dress on, Gisela had to admit it fit beautifully. The gown was made of fine fabric and the color suited her olive complexion, however, she wasn't sure how to keep her breasts from spilling over the top.

"We can push them down," the maid offered. It was obvious she fought not to laugh.

Lillian looked to explode with glee. "Nay! I have no doubt after today, ye will be overcome with men wishing to court ye."

"Mother, do not dare bring the subject up today. This is Verity's day." Gisela gave the maid a stern look. "Loosen the stays. I will pull the top up and ye will bind me in."

Finally after a few moments, her breasts were contained. She couldn't take a full breath, but that was preferable to looking like a tavern wench.

"There…now…that's better." Gisela sounded out of breath, but she didn't care.

"Are ye sure?" Her mother leaned in and studied her. "Can ye breathe?"

"Of course." Gisela plopped back down on the stool. "Pile my hair on top of my head and allow some curls to fall down the back," she instructed the maid, immediately regretting the long sentence. Her head began to spin and she let out what little breath came. It was going to be a long day.

Verity Ross and Patrick Munro stood at the front of the room with their hands bound together. Flushed and seeming delighted, Verity beamed up at her husband-to-be. Unlike his bride Patrick maintained the same lack of expression as during the last meal the day before.

Gisela couldn't sit, so she stood at the back of the room, her back against the wall. Practicing shallow breathing helped to keep her from fainting and she wondered if perhaps she should have come up with a better way to hide her bosom.

"Ye look about to pass out," Kieran whispered into her ear and she jumped at the deep voice. "Why do ye not sit?"

"Why are ye not at the front somewhere with yer family?" Gisela retorted. "I prefer to stand." She hitched her chin up.

"Suit yerself." He remained next to her, his attention to the front of the room.

Gisela took another short breath, blowing out the air slowly so, hopefully, he would not notice. Why did the man not go away?

Her mother turned and glanced at her and upon noticing Kieran, she smiled widely. Gisela looked up to the ceiling.

He had to have noticed her mother's reaction.

"Go away," she hissed to him.

"No. I prefer to stand here."

"What will ye do if my mother asks ye to marry me?" she said with a smirk. "She is very wily."

He looked to her out of the corners of his eyes. "She would not."

"Ye do not know my mother."

A woman seated near them turned and gave them a stern look. Gisela ignored her, keeping her eyes forward. It was best to save her energy to concentrate on breathing and disregard the stubborn man.

That was easier said than done as he caused a reaction within that was very hard to ignore, part of which was quickness of breath.

As soon as the couple was pronounced married, everyone spilled out of the chapel to either the great room or the courtyard. Gisela rushed directly to the far side of the keep to seek fresh air. She needed to loosen the binds or else she'd most definitely faint. The thought of going up the stairs took what little breath she had. So instead, with unsteady steps, she made her way to a far the corner of the garden.

Reaching behind her, she loosened the bindings and the bodice gaped open, allowing her to finally gulp in full breaths. "Goodness, this was a horrible idea," she muttered, never relishing air as much as she did at that moment.

It was only a few moments later that she realized it was impossible to tie the ribbons again. She tried wrapping them around her waist, but the bodice folded over, revealing her breasts. Next, she tried pulling up the chemise. It bunched up and made her look like a misshapen troll.

"Oh, no!" She held up the disheveled dress and took a step back into the shadows. "Why do I let my mother talk me into things."

She stepped onto a rock and peeked over the wall. The only person in view was a young guard. It was either get him to come and help or remain in the garden until dark. Then again, once people began to drink ale, no doubt a couple would come there to seek privacy and she'd be found out.

"Pssst!" Gisela made the sound and the guard looked around, but didn't see her. "Over here," she said. The young man's eyes narrowed in her direction.

"What do ye want?"

"I-I need help."

He walked closer, his gaze moving from her and then side-to-side. "With what?"

"I…er…well ye see, my dress, I need help tying it."

His brows fell. "Did Gavin put ye up to this?"

"Who? I do not know a Gavin."

"Mmm hmm." He walked backwards. "I am on duty and cannot. However, I can get a few other guards to come help ye."

"No!" Gisela called out louder than she meant. "Ye're right. It was Gavin. I will inform him ye did not fall for his jest."

The guard laughed and walked away, whistling.

Gisela lowered to the rock. "What to do now?"

There was rustling as someone stepped into the garden. Gisela froze and peered through low tree branches.

"I do not understand what exactly it is I can do. He does not respond to anything I have tried." Two women had approached, one older and the other younger. She knew them both from the village.

They were Maura and Angeline Finlay, mother and daughter. Maura's husband had died just recently. It was common knowledge that they were left without resources and had to sell many of their belongings to survive. Quite a sad state the poor women found themselves in.

Gisela's brother, Hamus, helped them with coin and other things, as he was sweet on Angeline. It seemed Maura didn't consider his help to be enough.

Knowing this was the woman his brother cared for made her move just a bit closer to hear better.

They didn't see her and Gisela's mouth fell open when Maura took her daughter by the arms and shook her.

"If ye cannot seduce him then ye must sneak into his bed and then cry out as if he is forcing himself upon ye. I will ensure there are witnesses so that he will then have no choice but to marry ye."

Angeline shook her head emphatically. "I cannot do that mother. Kieran Ross will be almost impossible to take unawares. Besides, he frightens me."

"Stop with the silliness. We need coin and a place to live. We are without resources."

"Hamus promised to see after us…"

"Nonsense. He has nothing to offer. A mere stable hand."

"I love him."

"Shut up," the older woman snapped and Gisela flinched.

"Mother, please," the young woman pleaded, her voice shaking.

"Do as I say. Ye must do it tonight, Angeline. Take a few moments to compose yerself," the woman hissed and stalked away.

Holding her bodice up to cover herself, she moved from her hiding place and neared the young woman who remained behind sniffing loudly.

"Angeline," Gisela said. Angeline jumped, her reddened eyes round like saucers. "We…I did not see ye."

"I need help." She motioned to her dress. "The maid bound my bodice much too tight. Unfortunately, I could not breath."

Angeline sniffed and nodded. "Of course I will help ye." She rounded Gisela, pulled up her bodice and chemise, bunching the fabric expertly. Soon, the dress was in place, the bunching of the chemise covering her perfectly.

"Thank ye," Gisela said and gave her an understanding look. "My mother is overzealous about finding me a husband as well. Is there anything I can do to help ye?"

"From what ye heard, ye know my mother will never accept yer brother as my husband." Angeline sniffed, her blue eyes wet with tears. "I do not wish to marry anyone but him."

"Then do so," Gisela said with a one-shouldered shrug. "Go fetch Hamus and tell him ye wish to marry immediately. My brother is too enamored with ye to allow what yer mother has planned to happen."

"He has already agreed to marry, but the laird has him in charge of all the horses and other clans' steeds for the wedding."

Gisela wanted to roll her eyes. "Very well. I will help and keep Kieran Ross from going to his chamber tonight. He will probably leave in the morning. Once this entire…" she waved her arm toward the courtyard, "…is over, ye and Hamus can get away and marry."

With that said, she slipped her arm through Angeline's. "I am glad ye will be my sister."

Angeline gave her a pretty smile. "Me as well."

As they entered the courtyard, Gisela spotted Kieran. Somehow, she'd find a way to keep him and Angeline from ending up in his chamber. First, she had to find out where he slept.

"Angeline, where is his chamber?"

"The last one on the second floor," Angeline replied. "On the right."

THE FESTIVITIES CONTINUED well into the evening. As tired as she was, Gisela needed to keep vigil over Kieran's movements. For the most part, he remained with his clansmen. The archers seemed to have a close camaraderie as loud laughter overtook them constantly. They sat at a table dragged away from the others on the opposite side of a large bonfire.

From where Gisela sat with her mother and a group of older

women, she could see Kieran clearly. He didn't join in the conversation, but she did see him laugh once. It was as if he'd caught himself because, right after, he'd scowled.

With the glow of the fire upon him, he was even more breathtaking than usual. His bow and quiver were strapped to his broad back. In a way, he seemed out of place, more like a person who lived in the forest.

Seeming to sense her perusal, his gaze moved toward her, but she looked away before their eyes could meet.

How would she keep him from going to his chamber to find Angeline there? Angeline's mother would do anything in her power to get her daughter to seduce Kieran, so it was up to Gisela to help.

"Gisela?" Her mother nudged her. "Go and fetch me something to drink please. I am parched."

THE MINX WAS up to something. Kieran could sense it. She'd kept an eye on him all through last meal. For some reason, she'd purposely walked past him, her skirts brushing against his back, as if signaling him. But when he'd turned, she walked back to her mother with a cup in hand and not paying him any attention.

"Yer lass is not seeming to pay ye much heed today," Tristan said with a smirk. "Did ye anger her?"

"She is not my lass," Kieran replied with a scowl. "Why do ye keep harping on."

Tristan shrugged. "She purposely brushed past ye and, even now, ye follow her every move."

What his brother said was true. "Because she is constantly doing something…" He stopped speaking and got to his feet. "I need fresh air." He stalked to the door, not looking back but hearing his brother snicker.

CHAPTER TEN

"WHAT ARE YE doing?"

The deep voice made Ceilidh whirl around and gasp. Ian's height hid the light of the sconce on the corridor wall and his shadow fell over her.

"Nothing, I am going in search of my wrap. It is a bit cold…" Taking a step backward, she could get a clearer view of his face.

His gaze traveled over her, the action causing her breathing to accelerate. "Why are ye here?"

"I owe ye an explanation." Ian spoke in a low tone that made his already deep voice seem even more so. "The way I ignored ye the last few weeks has not been fair."

Ceilidh remained silent, trying her best to work past the constriction in her throat. Although her eyes stung, she willed them to not tear up. She would not let this man know how deeply he'd hurt her.

The ache in her chest was worse than when he'd been gone or stayed out of her way. She wondered how long it would be before she'd be able to see him and not feel anything.

"Ye are a good woman who doesn't deserve…"

"Stop speaking!" Anger helped her speak out. "I understand. There is no need to say anything further." She held up both hands. "Now that ye are able and without injury, ye can aspire to more. Why would ye even consider a simple village woman like me?"

When an errant tear trickled down her cheek, she wanted to scream in annoyance.

Ian opened his mouth, but she slashed across the air with her right hand, silencing him. "I will get over ye, Ian McElroy, I will. But I beg ye to continue avoiding me. Tis best that way."

Before he could say another word, she turned away and raced to her chamber. Once there, she slammed the door, leaning against it. "I love ye." She slid to the floor, not caring about her beautiful new gown. Everything ached and she let the pain take over as she sobbed.

Tap. Tap. Tap. "Ceilidh." Ian had followed her.

"Go…go away."

"Not until ye listen."

She took a deep breath and shook her head to clear her thoughts. "Go away."

"I cannot leave until ye hear what I have to say. It is I who do not feel worthy of ye. How can I possibly bind ye to me, a man who is not whole and who ye could never be proud to stand next to?"

Eyes wide, Ceilidh could not believe what she was hearing. Ian did not feel worthy of her? The thought almost made her laugh.

"Have ye considered what will happen when I can no longer fight? Tis more possible for me to be hurt in battle now." He had to be pressing his mouth to the door for his words to come through so clearly.

She stood and went to the washbasin. The cool water felt good on her heated face. Hands trembling like leaves, Ceilidh ran them over her hair in an attempt to smooth any unruly locks.

After that, she walked to the door and opened it.

The vulnerability in Ian's expression almost made her cry again. His eyes bored into hers as if seeking answers without her speaking them.

Taking his hand, she pulled him into the room and then placed her hand on the center of his chest. He was the man she loved and he was perfect.

His broad chest lifted and lowered, and he stood very still, almost as if he were afraid to do something wrong.

Finally, Ceilidh looked up at him. "Ye are perfect. Yer heart and body are strong. I have no doubt ye would always defend me and overcome any obstacle to ensure that I am safe. Ye are a brave warrior who makes our laird proud."

"I am not sure…"

"Of course ye are. Ye remain in the guard because the men have no doubts about ye in battle. If it were different, they would ensure ye were sent to work elsewhere."

His gaze fell from hers to the floor and she hit him in the center of the chest. "Why do ye not believe the truth? Do ye to be filled with doubt?"

When she huffed, the corners of his lips twitched. "Ye are the one who is perfect, lass."

"If ye really feel that way about me, show me."

His mouth crashed over hers with such force that Ceilidh lost her breath. She reached around his neck and grasped his hair with her right hand.

His right arm wrapped around her waist, Ian pulled her tighter against him, never breaking the kiss.

Reason was gone and all Ceilidh could think of was taking him to her bed. She'd seen more than once how well formed he was, but to see and to touch were two very different things.

"Come to my bed," she gasped out when his mouth traveled down the side of her jaw to her throat. "I need ye."

"Are ye sure?" he murmured, his mouth barely lifting as he pressed kisses further down to the top of her breasts.

"Aye." The reply was breathless and it hung in the air, floating down over them as Ian continued kissing her while guiding her backward toward the small bed.

It took only a few moments to get rid of their clothing.

She fell back onto the bed and Ian came over her. Finally, she was pressed against him, skin to skin, the warmth of his body wonderful against the chill in the room.

Ceilidh welcomed his weight over her and let out a long sigh as she ran her hands down his broad back, enjoying the combination of the taut muscles and scars that reminded her of his vigor in battle.

Every sensation was new. Nothing in her life had prepared her for the feelings overtaking her at the moment, the press of his lips to different parts of her body, the lingering trails his tongue left as it traveled downward until he took first one tip of her breast in and then the other. When his fingers skittered over the overly sensitive skin of her inner thigh, a moan from deep in her throat rumbled out.

"Ian," she whispered, frantic to find out what happened next. The pleasure would culminate and come to an end. Of that, she was sure. Fear that it would end could not compete with the thought of what would happen next.

Doubt and thoughts about possible repercussions floated away when his fingers dipped between the folds of her sex and everything ceased to exist. Every part of her was lost as he began to circle her very center, sending heat down her legs and up to her core.

"Oh, what is this?" she cried out, too overcome to care to know if he responded or not. "Ahhhh."

His mouth took hers with urgency; perhaps to quiet her cries. And when the heat became more intense, she mewled in pleasure.

Just as she was about to fall to pieces, the pressure of his rod at her entrance brought her crashing down to the realization of what was about to happen and she lifted her hips, urging him on. Ian would take her that night and he would be hers forever.

She pushed away thoughts of the future. In that moment, all that mattered was joining with him.

Ian must have sensed a change because he hesitated, hovering just inside her. "Are ye sure?"

"Aye." Ceilidh pulled his face to her and took his mouth. "Take me."

When he pushed in, at first it was slowly, then he thrust hard, taking not only her maidenhead, but also her breath. Ceilidh cried out at the pain like that of being torn. Unsure what to do next, she took a trembling breath.

"Relax, my beauty. I will ensure it will be a memorable night. Trust me." Ian murmured the words into her ear as he moved in and out of her in a slow, rhythmic pace that soon took her mind away from the now gone ache. Instead, she marveled at his body and the way it moved.

Positioned between her legs, he used his right arm at the elbow and where the left one ended to hold his upper body up as he looked down at her, his hips rocking forward and back, his sex sliding within her and, soon, something began to happen. Her body tightened around him, coming to life with renewed need.

Ceilidh closed her eyes, but then opened them again, meeting his gaze. Her lips curved.

"Ye are worth more to me than any woman on this earth," Ian whispered and she believed he felt that way.

When his movements became frantic, Ceilidh was glad because she needed to find out what eluded her. She lifted her hips to match his thrusts and soon became lost once again. Suddenly, she floated into a place that was like no other and when the fall began, she let herself go.

"YE WILL BE my wife. I give ye no choice in the matter." Ian lay on his back with her splayed over him. "I mean it, Ceilidh. Do not argue with me."

She'd repeatedly told him she did not expect anything from him, but her protests had been weak. In truth, the fact he wanted to marry her was thrilling.

"One day, ye will speak in anger and say I trapped ye," she

said, pushing her finger into his chest. "And I will remind ye, I did not wish ye to feel forced to marry me."

His gaze met hers and her heart skipped. "There is nothing I wish for more than ye to be mine forever. Tis something I could not dare dream."

"Truly?" Ceilidh believed him. By the way he looked at her, as if nothing more precious ever existed, she knew he loved her.

"Aye."

"Very well," she replied and pressed a kiss to his lips. "I will marry ye, Ian."

He let out a satisfied grunt and chuckled. "Now, I have to figure out how to leave and go to my chamber without being seen."

"Tis better ye remain here tonight." Ceilidh lifted up and straddled him. "Ye said there was more ye could show me."

"True."

⤜⤜⤜✕⤛⤛⤛

"No!" Elspeth's rounded eyes met Ceilidh's. "Ye and Ian…"

"Shhh," Ceilidh whispered and tugged her friend out of the gate toward the flower field where they often walked. "If someone hears, it may go badly for him."

Her friend gave her a flat look. "Nothing will happen, other than perhaps Malcolm demanding he marry ye."

Laughter erupted. She was happy and could barely feel the ground beneath her feet. "Yer husband cares not about what happens between his guard and a simple village girl like me."

"Ye are my friend and companion. Anyone important to me is to him as well."

Considering the laird, Ceilidh shivered. He was a frightening man, who only showed a soft side when alone with her friend. Although she'd seen him do some things that could be considered nice, it was never enough to make her comfortable around him.

"When is the wedding?" Elspeth asked, her face bright. "It will be a great celebration. I will ask Moira to make a grand feast."

"Nay. Ian and I will marry in Kildonan. His mother will be an honored guest, not a servant."

Instantly, Elspeth realized her gaff. "I am so sorry. I forgot and did not think. Of course."

"Do not be upset," Ceilidh replied. "That ye want to do something special means a great deal to me. Of course, ye and the laird are to be there."

"Of course," Elspeth said with a wide smile. "But please allow us to help make it extra special. Ye are my closest friend, like a sister to me."

Ceilidh considered it. "Very well, but do not overdo it. Ian would not like it." She hesitated, her lips curving. "I suppose, first, I should ensure he has not changed his mind." Her stomach dipped at noticing the warrior headed toward them.

"Here comes the soon-to-be groom."

"Hush," Ceilidh said, her chest tightening.

Ian approached and nodded to Elspeth. "My lady."

"Ian," Elspeth said with a grin. "Ye make my sister very happy."

His gaze moved to Ceilidh. "I am undeserving of such a treasure."

"In that, we agree," Elspeth replied with a mischievous purse to her lips. "I do not think there is a man alive worthy of her. However, ye are who I would choose for her."

His expression softened at the compliment. "Thank ye, my lady."

"Now, I best head back and allow ye to speak about what hap…"

"I will be there shortly," Ceilidh interrupted and gave her friend a warning look.

Both watched as Elspeth walked away, humming.

"Ye have not changed yer mind about me then?" Ian asked, taking her hand. "I was afraid ye'd come to yer senses today and realize what a burden…"

"Stop." Ceilidh held her hand up to his mouth. "If anything, I would be the burden to ye. What happens to a guard who is forced to remain in his wife's bed too often and is late to report?"

Ian shook his head, the corners of his lips lifting. "I would not care." He leaned forward and kissed her. "I wish to marry ye as soon as possible and find out."

Ceilidh jumped up and down tugging at his right arm. "It should be in Kildonan, do ye not agree? The village women, my mother and aunts will wish to cook. Yer mother would be an honored guest. Elspeth and Malcolm…er our laird and lady will be there as well. They will insist on contributing and we will agree, but they will not be allowed to overdo it."

"I see ye have not given it much thought yet," Ian said, taking her around the waist and pulling her against him as he took her mouth. This time with a bit too much passion as they were within sight of the keep guards.

Ceilidh wrapped her arms around his neck, not caring one bit.

CHAPTER ELEVEN

KIERAN LEFT LAST meal as soon as he finished eating and headed outdoors. First thing in the morning, he would continue his quest to find Ethan McLeod. There had been too many delays and, admittedly, he'd allowed himself to be distracted by not just his family but also Gisela. What the lass did or didn't do had little to do with him. Other than the effect she had on him, there was nothing to tie him to remain there any longer.

In truth, he'd grown fond of her and was genuinely intrigued, but she was a distraction he could not allow. There were too many risks to becoming involved, the timing was wrong.

As it stood, what happened after he got his revenge was not clear. It could be it would be a match to the death for both of them. He was prepared and didn't care if death claimed him, as long as he killed Ethan first.

Kieran marched through the courtyard toward the stables. Once the saddle packs were filled with what he needed, it would make leaving at dawn easier.

There were still many people about, the wedding festivities continuing. His sister seemed happy and he was glad for it.

"It will be good to return home," his cousin, Ruari, said upon seeing him. "Too many McLeods in the last days for my tastes."

"Aye, tis true. I seek only one, not to be surrounded by them."

Ruari studied him for a moment. "He has avoided being caught for months now, leading ye in circles. I fear avenging yer father's death will not bring ye the satisfaction ye think it will."

"What would ye know of that?" Kieran snapped and then realized that Ruari had lost his father when he was very young. The one responsible had been caught and executed by the clan.

His cousin shook his head. "I replay that day when my father's killer died. I have felt many things, but never satisfaction. I wanted nothing more than for my da to return to me."

"Forgive me. I didn't think," Kieran said, not wishing to continue the conversation. There was no reasoning that would stop him from pursuing the need for vengeance, nor anyone that could stop him.

Ruari met his gaze and Kieran could see understanding in his cousin's eyes. "Ye should go and do what ye have to do, but know it will only be a salve. Tis only time that will soothe the pain and only the passing of years that will bring ye to one day wake without the burden of guilt weighing ye down."

His stomach clenched as if Ruari had punched him and Kieran physically flinched. The yoke of guilt and resentment did, indeed, weigh heavy and it was through sheer willpower that he got out of bed every morning. His only motivations were rage, anger and the need to see life ebb from Ethan McLeod.

"I will leave at dawn. Be with care, Cousin," Kieran spoke as he finished stashing the last of the items into the bags and then walked back out of the stables.

Ruari had remained quiet, for there was nothing to be said. Nothing that would make Kieran change his mind and stay there with the family. Both men knew this.

The activity in the courtyard had lessened as people began seeking a place to sleep. Kieran considered staying in the stables, but he had to speak to his sister and mother and inform them of his departure.

In the great room, he found both of them. Verity waved her hands in the air as she spoke. It had been a long time since he'd seen both his sister and mother so animated and happy. A part of him resented how easy the transition of losing his father seemed to be for them.

"I leave at dawn," he interrupted without preamble. "I will ensure to stop by here upon my return."

His mother's eyes narrowed. "Who goes with ye?"

"I am going north. Alone."

"That will not do at all. That madman is out there, he could ambush ye." His mother turned and waved Tristan over.

Kieran wanted to roll his eyes but refrained. "I would welcome that he do it. It would make it easier for me to kill him."

"Ye have no idea how many men travel with him. What if he has a small army? Ye could be killed and I would not be informed."

"Ye would know eventually," Kieran replied and let out a long breath when Tristan and another guard neared. "I do not need anyone to go with me."

Tristan frowned, his expression dark. "Ye are scaring our mother with yer intent to go on a fool's quest if ye go alone."

He'd made a mistake. He should have kept silent.

"We must talk." Tristan pulled him aside and spoke in a lowered voice. "What if ye are walking into a trap? Have ye stopped and wondered why it is so easy to know where he is at times? He is toying with ye."

"I do not care. There is nothing ye can do to stop me."

Tristan looked over his shoulder and four guards arrived. Not touching any part of Kieran's body, they surrounded him and walked as a group through the great room.

Once they reached the top of the stairs, Kieran decided he'd had enough. He whirled around. "Do ye plan to place guards outside my bedchamber?"

"Nay," Tristan said, "but they will be at the stables to keep ye from leaving."

His teeth set, Kieran stared at the men's retreating backs as they went back down the stairs. Being the youngest brother his entire life, Kieran had become adept at stealing away and doing things prohibited by his parents. This would be an ultimate test of his abilities.

"Rest, Brother. We will travel north to hunt down Ethan McLeod. But ye will not go alone. I will see to it. Nothing good can come from it."

His brother followed after the guards and Kieran could barely keep from driving his fist against the nearest wall.

Nothing about what happened changed his plans. In the morning, he would mount his horse and leave. Guards or no guards, they would not stop him.

"Ye cannot go into yer chamber." A familiar voice made him swing around to see Gisela looking up at him, a furrow between her brows.

He'd hoped to avoid seeing her that evening and it had been relatively easy until then.

Kieran scowled down at her. "Move aside, Gisela. I am in no mood to speak to anyone right now."

"I require yer help with…"

"No."

"If ye would just listen to me…"

"I said no."

Her gaze moved from him to the doorway. "Very well, I will tell ye what is about to happen…"

He took her arm and moved her aside. "Whatever foolishness ye have to spout, say it to someone else."

The shocked expression made him want to take the words back, but he couldn't bring himself to do so. It was for the best that she be angry with him. If she was hurt, perhaps she would not want anything to do with him again.

The night had grown progressively worse, he considered, as he walked into the dark chamber. Without lighting a candle, he yanked his tunic off and then kicked off his boots. He went to the bed and fell upon it.

There was a sound like that of a soft gasp. He listened. It probably came from the open window, perhaps someone spending time with a woman.

In this moment, he had to keep his mind on the goal. His goal was to get away at first light and head north.

Upon arriving at the northern post, he would begin tracking his prey. He could almost smell the bastard. Ethan McLeod was not far.

His lips curved at considering that soon he would kill the man and his thirst would be quenched.

Just as his eyes fell closed, there was movement. "Make love to me," the voice quivered and he pushed away.

"Get out of my bed," he growled out, "or else I will toss ye into the corridor."

The woman began to cry and he sat up in the bed. Reaching for the woman, he took her by the arm. But just as he was about to climb out of the bed dragging her with him, someone called out from the doorway.

"What is the meaning of this?" A woman stood just inside his chamber and held up a lantern. "How dare ye take advantage of my daughter in such a manner?"

Kieran growled in annoyance. This was not the first time someone had tried this particular trick to force him into marriage.

The woman at the doorway cried out theatrically. "Ye have my daughter in yer bed." Turning to the hallway, she continued. "Oh, no, what shall we do." With each word, the lantern swung in her hand, sending light in all directions.

"Get out of my bed," Kieran growled to the younger woman who remained next to him, looking at the older woman with terror-filled eyes. He got out of the bed and pulled on his tunic. "Now!"

"I am sorry," she whispered. "I do not wish…"

The older woman stomped closer and let out a bloodcurdling scream. "This is most upsetting. My daughter is ruined," she cried out.

"Both of ye, leave my chamber at once," Kieran said, furious now. The scheme would not work and even if he had to, he'd drag both out and toss them into the corridor.

"What is happening?" His mother of all people hurried in, her eyes widening at the young woman in his bed. "Son? Who is this?"

"I do not know. I've never seen her before," he replied in a bored tone. Although he'd been through this before, his mother had never been involved.

His mother's eyes narrowed at the woman holding the lantern. "Why are ye and yer daughter in my son's chamber?"

The older woman huffed. "I heard my daughter cry out. Yer son was forcing himself upon her."

Kieran rolled his eyes and prepared to leave the room. He'd find another place to sleep. It was almost comical that the young woman remained in his bed, seeming confused as to what to do next.

"I did not force myself on her and neither will I marry her. I walked in just a moment ago, alone. Right before this woman." He motioned to the woman who continued to hold up the lantern. "My brother and guards will attest to it."

The older woman didn't seem at all deterred by his statement. Although she cowered next to his mother, she tried to put up a brave front. "Ye shall make this right, Kieran Ross."

He crossed both arms over his chest. "Tis not the first time someone has tried to trap me in this manner." Kieran looked to the girl who looked back at him with hopeful eyes. She did not wish to marry him either.

"Tis not a bad idea that ye marry. This would be a good thing for ye. Settle ye down. I am sure this girl comes from a good family." His mother finally decided to speak and he rewarded her with a glower.

He turned to the woman in the bed who silently urged him to

fight what was happening and then once again faced her mother. "Ye are a foolish woman." He grabbed his sword, bow and quiver, and his boots from the floor and slid one last glance to the women who watched in silence.

"Get out of my way."

The women scrambled sideways when he stormed past. It had been a long time since he'd been so annoyed.

In stockinged feet, he hurried down a stairwell.

"This is not the last of it," the woman with the lantern followed, her shrill voice making him cringe.

There were a few people in the great room, mostly men sleeping on the floor. When he turned a corner, Gisela walked toward him carrying folded linens. She'd obviously been helping settle guests.

"I hope to receive an invitation to yer wedding." She brushed past him, her shoulder bumping his arm.

She'd known about the plan to trap him and had tried to stop him. Kieran considered chasing after her, but then realized it would be foolish. Being caught in a room with one woman this night was more than enough. Besides, the screeching woman remained at the top of the stairs.

The night air cooled his face as Kieran headed to the stables. He'd find a cot or a free space on the floor there and sleep until he could get away.

IT WAS STILL dark when Kieran rode away from Munro Keep. He'd had enough of being around people and being deterred from his goal.

After knocking out one guard and sneaking past a sleeping one, his escape had been relatively easy.

Content to be away from being stabled, his mount didn't need much encouragement to gallop and soon they were well away from Munro lands.

Once again, his body hummed with the need for revenge. The blood in his veins coursed through him so hard that his heart thundered in his ears. Every sense on high alert, he studied the surroundings. There wasn't anything that would ever stop him from killing Ethan McLeod. Except maybe his own death.

Hours later, at a slower pace, Kieran made his way through the outskirts of Ross lands that bordered on the Mackenzie's and guided his mount to a creek and dismounted.

The surroundings seemed undisturbed by humans and not traveled through recently.

Once he relieved himself and washed his hands and face in the cool water, he fed his horse and looked about for a good place to settle for the night. The moon was bright in the darkened sky, giving him enough light to see clearly.

There was no need to hurry as he'd lost his prey by remaining at Munro Keep for so many days. He'd go to the northern post that was guarded by Ross guards and get a report of any sightings and then continue from there.

Moments later, Kieran lay on a roll of blankets, his gaze traveling past the treetops to the sky. Where was the bastard? If Ethan hunted him, he had to be near. After all, news of Verity's wedding was known to the McLeods.

Different scenarios playing in his head, Kieran fell asleep.

Moments later, even before seeing them, he heard the approaching footsteps.

Three men surrounded him swords drawn.

Kieran's hand tightened around the hilt of his own weapon that he kept next to him.

"Who are ye?"

He gave the bearded man who asked a flat stare. "Kieran Ross."

Then all went dark.

CHAPTER TWELVE

"COME AT ONCE," Lillian demanded, waking Gisela from a deep slumber. "We have much to do."

Gisela sat up and rubbed her eyes. "Ye mean pack our clothes and leave?"

Her mother studied a skirt and then pushed it back into the trunk. "Don't be silly. Today, I can finally speak to Laird Munro about a husband for ye. The wedding is over."

"Mother, why do ye not seek a husband for yerself? I will find one on my own. I do not require yer assistance, nor do I wish to be ordered to marry someone I do not desire."

Her mother's lips curved. "Desire. It has been so long since I…"

"Never mind that," Gisela interrupted. "Let us break our fast and seek out a wonderful man for ye. I will help."

Distracted by the idea, her mother rushed to the doorway and hesitated. "I need a maid to assist me. I must look my best today."

Thankfully, her mother remained self-absorbed and could easily be deterred by turning things around to be about her.

Gisela hurried and dressed. Since the maid who'd been summoned would be busy with her mother, she did her own hair, brushing it back into a simple bun at the nape of her nape.

"Mother, I will go downstairs and seek out a perfect place to sit and break our fast," she said from the door.

Her mother waved happily. "Make sure that we are visible from every doorway."

When she exited the room, Gisela let out a breath and went to the great room.

There were still plenty of people but it wasn't hard to find empty seats at a small table where an older couple sat drinking from their cups with bored expressions.

"Good morning," Gisela greeted brightly and immediately the elderly couple lit up.

"Well, aren't ye a beauty," the woman said and gave her husband a knowing look.

"Aye, quite so," he agreed. "What is yer name?"

The conversation remained pleasant and Gisela was glad for her choice of seats. Not only was the couple quite nice, but they were indeed in perfect view of every entrance.

There was a lull in the conversation and heads pivoted toward the room's indoor entrance.

Gisela forced herself to look to the stairwell. Like a queen, halfway down the stairs, her mother paused for effect. In a dress that was much too revealing for so early in the day, her bosom was barely concealed. She'd donned a shawl, but it hung from the edges of her shoulders. Admittedly, her hairstyle, piled atop her head allowing for her long neck to show, was becoming. Lillian Munro walked regally down the rest of the steps and through the room.

The women in the room exchange astonished looks at her mother's lack of decorum, but the men in the room didn't seem at all bothered.

As exasperating as the display was, her mother was youthful and it would not be hard for Gisela to find a man to keep her preoccupied. Gisela scanned the room until finding one man in particular who watched intently as Lillian crossed the room.

With silver sideburns and dressed well, it was obvious he wasn't a warrior, but perhaps a merchant. He would be her target.

"May I present my mother," Gisela said to the older couple at the table. The woman's eyes rounded and the man didn't bother looking up past her mother's exposed skin.

Once Lillian sat, the woman was won over by her mother's sense of humor and, soon, the couple pronounced they were thrilled at having someone sit and speak to them.

After a few moments, Gisela stood and made her way to the back of the great room. Once she neared the man who'd watched her mother earlier, she stopped. "My mother wishes to speak to ye."

The man's eyebrows rose. "She does?"

"Aye, ye see, we need assistance going home and hope ye can find it in yer heart to take us."

He didn't ask any other question of her, but hurried to the table where her mother sat.

With a satisfied smile, she hurried out of the room toward the kitchens.

"Gisela." Angeline neared. "Thank ye for trying."

"What happened?"

Angeline shrugged. "Other than being made a fool of, nothing really." They walked out the back door. "He refused to be forced into anything. Quite a frightening man." Angeline shivered. "His mother told us he was untamable."

"It sounds about right," Gisela replied. "What will ye do now?"

"I plan to speak to Hamus and insist we marry right away. He can continue to work here and there is naught my mother can do."

They walked toward the stables just as Tristan Ross exited and stalked to them.

"Goodness, he is quite large," Angeline said with a worried expression. "Is he coming to speak to us?"

The warrior pinned Gisela with glare. "Where is Kieran?"

"How would I know?" Gisela snapped. "I have not seen him today."

Tristan's hazel gaze moved past her to the keep. "Did he tell ye of his plans?"

Instinctively, Gisela knew Kieran was gone. He'd left and, in all probability, it would be a long time before she ever saw him again. Her heart dropped at considering her life without seeing him.

"Nay, he has no reason to." Gisela walked away from Tristan, not waiting to hear anything else.

Chest tight, she accompanied Angeline in search of Hamus. Her brother was at the corral gates, leading a horse in.

"Have ye seen Kieran Ross?" Gisela asked him.

"He left early, before sunrise," he replied. Then at seeing Angeline, his face lit up.

Gisela walked closer to Hamus and pushed a finger into his chest. "While ye are delaying things, Angeline was forced upon him by her mother last night."

Angeline gasped and Hamus growled. "What happened?"

Moving her aside, Angeline explained her mother's plan and how it had failed. The expressions that crossed her brother's face made it plain to Gisela that he would agree to marry Angeline quickly.

Leaving them to be alone, she made her way back to the house. Once the merchant escorted her and her mother back to the village, she would return to her cottage. Although it was a lonely life, it was peaceful. Perhaps in the near future, she would seek a husband. But at the moment, the constant thoughts of Kieran would make it unfair for any man.

With a deep sigh, she meandered, not in a hurry to go back into the stifling interior.

A maid hurried to her. "There ye are. Lady Munro wishes to speak to ye. She said it is about a pending matter."

"Oh...oh, no." Gisela wondered if it had to do with marriage between her and Caylen.

"I will be there shortly," Gisela replied, looking toward the gates.

"Lady Munro insisted ye come with me."

As she followed the maid, Gisela racked her brain to come up with a way out of the predicament.

Lady Munro sat with another woman Gisela had seen about, but didn't know. The woman's gaze traveled down her body before lifting up to meet her eyes. Obviously, she was being measured for potential wife material.

Gisela assumed a bored look before bowing. "Lady Munro, ye require me for something?"

"I would like ye to meet my dear friend, Frances Roberts. She has a son that requires a wife and yer mother made it clear ye are anxious to marry."

Frances' cold accessing eyes met Gisela's. "Do ye cook? Sew?"

Why was everyone intent on controlling her life? "I prefer to eat whatever grows on trees. I detest cooking. As for sewing, I take whatever needs mending to my friend who is a seamstress. Tis easier." She scratched her head. "Does yer son cook?"

The woman's eyes widened and then narrowed. She knew that Gisela was doing her best to dissuade them.

"I'd prefer a likable young woman for my son. This one is not in the least trying to be accommodating."

Lady Munro laughed and winked at Gisela. "She is delightful, but quite strong-willed." Shaking her head, she waved Gisela away. "I think ye will have to find a husband on yer own sweet girl."

It was hard not to like Lady Munro who was always in good spirits. Gisela grinned back at her.

"I was about to seek ye and ask if ye'd like to join me for a trip to the village." Lady Munro had looked past her and spoke to whoever had entered.

Gisela turned to find herself looking at Kieran's mother. Lady Ross seemed stern, but then again, so was her son.

Lady Ross looked to Lady Munro. "I would be delighted." She then met Gisela's gaze. "Ye are a Munro, are ye not?"

"Aye." Gisela got a sinking feeling in her stomach. Not another attempt to get her married off, she hoped.

"I hear good things about ye. Tristan and the rest of the Ross party travel back to Ross Keep. Ye should go with them. Tis time for that son of mine to settle and from what I hear, he is quite smitten with ye."

"Oh, that would be lovely. I will order her things packed immediately," her mother said, appearing out of nowhere. "We have not formally met. I am Lillian Munro," she announced at noting Lady Ross.

"My husband's brother's wife," Lady Munro added with an indulgent smile. "The beautiful lass is my niece, Gisela."

"Oh, yes, I know who she is." Lady Ross said. "Tis my hope that once settled, Kieran will come to live on our lands which border near here. What better reason than having a Munro for a wife?" She scowled. "Better than any McLeod will ever be."

Kieran would not marry her. He would never be forced into something he did not wish to do. How would she recover from it, his blatant refusal? Her heart would be broken regardless of how much she wished to deny it.

Gisela let out a long sigh and left the room as they older women discussed her future. She trudged to the courtyard.

Unfortunately, there were Ross guards everywhere. They'd be traveling back to their lands that day and were busy preparing horses and such.

She considered sneaking away on foot, but her village and home were on the way to Ross lands. They'd pass right by there. She could not hide anywhere. Accepting defeat, she let out a sigh and turned back to go inside.

Kieran was gone to hunt for the man he wanted to kill and would probably be away for a long time. He would not be forced to marry anyone, so upon his return, she'd tell him there was no need and insist he bring her home.

Her lips curved. She'd not give him the opportunity to reject her in front of everyone. Instead, she would reject him. Openly anyway. What could be better? A trip to a place she'd never been before. Meeting new people and then, after a while, returning home.

With renewed energy, she went to oversee the packing of her belongings.

CHAPTER THIRTEEN

TIED TO A tree with his arms pulled back, Kieran did his best to get comfortable. His horse had ambled off and the damned robbers had left with his sword. His bow and quiver had been thrown into the creek and they'd left without a care of what would happen to him.

His arms were numb, but he'd managed to loosen the rope just a bit. He blew out a breath and whistled, hoping his horse, Laith, would hear and return. The horse didn't and he wondered if perhaps the damned animal had gone too far to hear him.

Kieran did his best to fight the anguish at the idea of losing the animal. Admittedly, he loved the animal that'd been his constant companion for so many years.

A noise woke him later that day, his stiff neck protesting with each movement. Kieran rolled his shoulders and, once again, attempted to loosen the bindings. They held fast. Would this be how he would die? Starve to death tied to a damned tree?

There was rustling in the leaves and a pair of deer appeared. Kieran rolled his eyes when they looked to him with curiosity. At least it wasn't a wild boar or a bear.

The sky was clear as the sun rose directly overhead and he cringed upon realizing he needed to relieve himself.

With a loud growl, he struggled with renewed energy. The deer scampered away and his wrists burned.

Ding. Ding. Ding. Bells woke Kieran and he craned his neck to look around the tree. It sounded as if a peddler traveled near.

"Who goes there?" he called out. "Can ye help me?"

At the sound of nearing footsteps, Kieran prepared himself for what could be another bad encounter.

"Over here," he called out.

"What do we have here?" A craggy-faced man peered down at him. "Got yerself in quite a quandary." The man waved a gnarled finger at him. "Tis not the first time someone tried this trick on me." He looked around as if expecting people to jump out from behind trees.

"I was robbed and left here," Kieran said in a flat tone.

"It seems to me, the fates are against ye," the old man stated, staring into the bonfire they'd made. Kieran's shoulders and arms remained sore from being tied to a tree for an entire day and night and his wrists smarted from the rope cuts. He was definitely not in the mood for conversation.

However, he owed the man for releasing him and allowing him to travel in his wagon.

At the slow pace the man traveled, it would be a fortnight before they reached a destination where he could contact his family.

"What happened had more to do with my lack of being alert than the fates," Kieran grumbled. "Do ye think it is possible to get to Kildonan tomorrow?"

The man scratched his beard in thought. "That is a grand idea. I have always sold well there. Indeed, we shall make it our goal. However, my mule is quite stubborn and refuses to go faster some days."

Resigned to the fact, he had little choice but to wait. Kieran studied the mule, which seemed content to stand still and look into the trees.

"How many times have ye been robbed?"

The man shrugged. "Thanks be to God, not too many. I have been beaten a few times and had coins taken, but they take one look at Gus and leave him behind." The man chuckled. "Little do they know, but his looks are deceiving. He is a strong and young beast."

Kieran cringed at considering his horse. The animal would hopefully remain in the area where he'd been robbed when he returned to search for him.

THANKFULLY, THEY DID arrive at Kildonan at dusk the following day. After thanking the man and promising him a reward if he came to Dun Airgid, Kieran hurried in search of the Elspeth's father, the town blacksmith.

Within an hour, he was on his way home with a new sword. He would stay home long enough to fashion a new bow and ensure he had enough arrows. Additionally, he would pack foodstuffs and whatever else had to be replaced. Along with his quest to find Ethan, now he hoped to find his horse.

Interestingly, he did not feel at all put off by his situation. Perhaps what the peddler had stated was correct. There was a reason he'd been brought back to Ross lands. It could be his enemy was near.

He bit into bread that Elspeth's mother had packed for him and drank from a wineskin. Ensuring to keep a sharp lookout for anyone approaching, Kieran urged his mount to a steady pace. He would not allow anyone to sneak up on him this time.

Without his bow and quiver, it was as if a part of him were missing. The last set he'd had for many years. But he refused to think on what the items meant to him. There was naught that could be done about it.

When Dun Airgid came into view, he let out a breath. Within moments, mounted guards lined up in front of the gates and two rode out toward him. Upon recognizing him, they relaxed.

"What happened to ye?" Of all people, it was Naill who asked.

Kieran did not wish to speak of his circumstances, especially not to Naill, whom he did not care for at all. "Has the party from Munro lands returned?"

"Aye. Just yesterday," Naill replied. "Yer betrothed came as well."

He scowled. No doubt his mother had agreed to him marrying the woman who'd tried to trap him. "I am not betrothed."

"That is what the lass said as well," Naill replied, making Kieran curious that the man was actually holding a conversation with him.

He decided a conversation with Naill was not intolerable. "Any news?"

"Nay, other than everyone has been worried since yer horse returned without ye. Search parties were sent out this morning to search for ye."

Kieran rolled his eyes. "Interesting that I did not see anyone the entire way here."

Naill glowered. No doubt the men who'd been sent out were his men. "They went north. What direction did ye come from?"

"North."

They continued toward the keep in silence. Kieran was glad to hear Laith was back. He'd not been relishing the idea of training a new horse to his ways, plus Laith was almost like a friend.

As they passed through the gates into the courtyard, he was greeted by quiet. There were only a few people about. Two stable lads hurried toward him.

"Brush down the horse, feed and water him." Kieran turned to Naill. "Can ye send two men to return the horse to Kildonan? It belongs to Elspeth's father."

Naill nodded. "Of course."

"Thank ye," Kieran said.

Naill's eyebrows hitched. "Ye're welcome."

Unsure of what to do first, he decided it was best to eat, rest and then see about clean clothing. The next day, he'd make a bow and get arrows.

He stalked into the great room. Malcolm sat at the front of the room, people before him as he presided over the needs of the clan. Tristan stood with the council in deep conversation in front of a large hearth.

There were a few people waiting to speak to Malcolm but, for the most part, it was a quiet day. Then again, it was late afternoon and whoever had been heard that morning had probably already departed.

"Kieran," Malcolm called out, getting to his feet and meeting him halfway. "Tis good to see ye are well." The look of genuine concern on his eldest brother's face made Kieran relax enough to allow the tight hug that followed.

"I was sure something terrible had happened to ye." Once again, his brother took stock, his gaze moving over him. "Are ye hurt?"

"I am well," he mumbled. "Got robbed. Lost my bow and quiver."

"Were ye harmed?" Tristan had walked up and studied his face. "Got banged up a bit, aye?"

He was aware of purpling around his left eye, his split lip and bruised jaw, but he hadn't taken the time to think about it before then. Once again, he was enveloped into a tight hug.

"Ye cannot hope to find Ethan alone. We must put together a party." Malcolm guided him away from the others to stand near the hearth. Two hounds that slept, warmed by the fire, lifted their heads. One wagged his tail lazily before settling back to continue its nap.

Kieran scowled at the dog. "These hounds are not good at guarding."

"True." His brother looked down at the dogs. "They earn their keep in other ways."

Unless tripping people was a job, Kieran couldn't think of anything the dogs did. But like his brothers, he would never mistreat the animals that had belonged to their father.

"A party will not help us in finding the bastard. I think he traveled north in an effort to find me," Kieran said. "But too much time has passed. Scouts have to be sent to investigate."

"I have sent men out. Hopefully, one will bring news soon. Tis best for ye to remain here until then."

Kieran nodded, aware it would be foolish to leave without hearing what news the scouts would bring. "How long?"

"Any day now. They've been gone for five days at least."

He would wait. Looking about the room, he hated being there. Whenever he was home, it was a stark reminder of his father's absence. "How do ye do it?"

Malcolm met his gaze with understanding. "Tis the best way to honor him. To take care of his people." Letting out a long breath, Malcolm placed a hand on Kieran's shoulder. "Ye do realize killing Ethan McLeod will not ease the burden ye carry."

"It will help." Kieran turned to a servant, who took two steps backward. He wanted to roll his eyes.

Malcolm chuckled. "Perhaps if ye didn't scowl so much, they would be more at ease."

"Is Moira in the kitchen?" he asked the wide-eyed maid who nodded. Annoyed, he stalked to the kitchen. Moira would feed him and then he would spend time at sword practice.

"Sweet boy, what happened to ye?" The cook rushed to him, tugging him to a chair. She turned to a young woman who looked about to swoon. "Bring a pot of hot water and some cloths." Moira studied his face. "Yer lip is bleeding."

"Aye, it splits every time I talk," he replied, glad to be in the confines of the kitchen and away from everyone. As a little boy, he'd always found the kitchen comforting, a refuge of sorts. He'd spent endless days there, often playing with Moira's son, Ian, by the fireplace.

Moira cleaned his face and began threading a needle. He winced even before she began to stitch the cut that went from the end of his mouth, across to his cheek. A couple kicks to his face had given him quite a bruising.

A few stitches later and salve placed on his cuts, she fed him chicken stew with carrots and buttered bread. He ate his fill, almost reluctant to stand and go outside.

"I met yer betrothed. She is quite lovely."

"Who?" He stood at the doorway.

"The girl who came back with Tristan from the wedding."

He'd all but forgotten about the incident. "I am not getting married."

"She's in the garden with Lady Elspeth and Ceilidh." Moira neared with a wide smile.

"Oh, ye don't know the great news. Ian and Ceilidh are to marry."

"I am glad to hear it," Kieran said, meaning it.

He walked out to seek the guards and practice. After he practiced, he'd see Ruari about making a bow. As he walked out, Kieran peered toward the garden. Four women went about the task of weeding and such. His brothers' wives and the girl, Ceilidh, moved about with baskets, all wearing long aprons. The fourth was familiar, too, and not at all who he expected.

What was Gisela doing there?

CHAPTER FOURTEEN

G ISELA SENSED HIM before seeing him. She looked up to see Kieran walking away. Had he seen her?

"What do ye think?" Merida, the wife of Tristan Ross, touched Gisela's shoulder.

"About?" She'd stopped listening upon seeing Kieran. Had he seen her? If so, why didn't he come and speak to her. Ask why she was there?

Merida let out a sigh, her gaze moving past Gisela to where Tristan had gone. "He's here." Her brow fell into a scowl. "I do not care for him at all."

"Why not?" Gisela prepared to hear that he'd been a scoundrel, a man without care of how he treated women.

Just then, Elspeth neared and looked to them both. "My opinion of Kieran Ross is that he carries a heavy burden of guilt and anger. He is directing it toward the McLeods but, in reality, the person he blames the most for Laird Ross' death is himself."

"What ye say is true. Therefore, I do my best to avoid him. No matter that I am his brother's wife, I do not trust Kieran in the least." Merida huffed and turned away to continue her chores.

Elspeth, wife to the laird, a man almost as imposing as Kieran, shook her head. "What do ye plan to say to him?"

"I will ask that he take me back to my village. He no more wishes to marry me than I do him." Gisela frowned. "Do ye think he would harm Merida?"

"Nay. I do not." Elspeth studied her for a moment. "Nor do I believe ye do not care for him. Marriage may be just what he needs to help him settle."

The last thing Gisela expected was that Kieran's family would want him to marry. "Ye know as well as I do he won't do anything he doesn't wish to. Even once his vendetta is done, Kieran Ross will continue to carry that burden. Ye said so yerself."

Her new friend looked crestfallen. "Tis sad, is it not?"

Gisela nodded. "Aye."

As the sun lowered, Gisela ambled to the herb shed. She'd tied herbs in bundles and now would hang them up to dry. Only Ceilidh remained outside. Elspeth had gone to see about last meal and Merida had left with Tristan, who'd come to collect her.

Ceilidh talked nonstop about her betrothed, which lightened Gisela's heart. When the one-armed warrior had come to the gate, the woman had practically floated to greet him. They'd exchanged a few words and he'd given her a quick kiss before Ceilidh had remembered Gisela.

"Ian, this is Gisela. Perhaps ye have met."

The handsome warrior looked to her and nodded. "I saw ye at Munro Keep, did I not?"

"Aye," Gisela nodded smiling.

Once he left, promising to sit with Ceilidh at last meal, the woman began talking again about their wedding plans.

"Ye are invited, of course. It will be at my village, Kildonan."

"Thank ye, but I doubt I will be here that long."

"Where do ye think to be?" Kieran asked, walking through the open gate. His gaze clashed with hers. By the deep scowl, he was furious.

Ceilidh darted away and into the kitchen, leaving her alone. Obviously, everyone was terrified of the man.

"Home, of course." Gisela hitched her chin.

"Then why are ye here?"

She blew out a breath. "Because everyone is bent on marrying me off. Ye were there, do ye not remember? Once ye left, I was forced to come here."

Eyes narrowed, he seemed to ponder over her words. "Ye could have escaped. Did ye even try?"

Despite the fact she'd not planned to marry him, the fact he was not willing to even consider it hurt. She did her best to blink back tears and ignore the tightening in her chest. "Can ye order guards to take me home? I do not wish to remain anywhere near yer presence."

She attempted to go around him, but he took her arm. "Where are ye going?"

"Away from ye." Horror filled Gisela when tears trickled down her cheeks. "I am tired of having to fight for my independence. Everyone thinks they have power over me. Why can I not be left alone to do as I please, live as I wish?"

She took a shaky breath. "I do wish to marry one day, to a men who cares for me. A man of honor."

His face turned to stone. "I see."

Her shoulders slumped. "Please…take me…home." Gisela hiccupped through the sentence. "I just wish to be…home." It was as if a wave hit her, making it impossible to fight the tide. Gisela began to sob.

And the most unexpected thing happened. Kieran pulled her against him and held her as she wept into his tunic.

She didn't move away from him because, for the first time, there was only protection and security. Not since her father had it felt that the man who held her would ensure no harm would come to her. If only he would never let go.

"I am so scared," she finally admitted. "What will happen to me?"

Kieran's chest rose and lowered. "I do not know. I can make arrangements to ensure ye are taken back to yer cottage. That will not stop yer mother from seeking a husband for ye."

Afraid he'd move away, she clutched the rough fabric of his tunic. "Aye, I only fool myself to think I have any power over what happens to me."

She released his clothing and stepped back. "Please, do so. I would like to return home."

For a long moment, he studied her face and then abruptly turned and walked away without replying.

During last meal, Gisela sat with Ceilidh. Besides Ceilidh, Elspeth and Merida seemed to assume she'd remain there and marry Kieran. It was laughable since he'd barely looked in her direction. But she didn't argue the fact since it would do little good.

Once arrangements were made for her to return home, everyone would be aware the wedding would not take place.

"Besides ye, Moira is the only woman here that dares go near him," Ceilidh said, her gaze shifting to where Kieran was sitting.

He leaned toward the cook as she spoke to him and nodded. When she shook a finger at him, Gisela's eyes widened. Whatever exchange was happening between him and the older woman, it was as if he were being chastised in some manner.

When Moira walked off, he looked in Gisela's direction and then quickly away. Had Moira spoken to him about her? It was probably something he'd done to upset the cook that had nothing to do with her.

At the head table, Elspeth had watched the exchange and hid a smile behind her hand. She leaned over her husband and said something to Merida, who then looked to Gisela.

"Whatever is afoot, I believe it has to do with me," Gisela whispered to Ceilidh. The woman simply nodded.

"I was about to say the same."

The mood during the evening meal remained constrained, almost as if someone or something was expected. Several times, Gisela caught people looking to the doorway and then around the room as if trying to figure out what was going to happen.

She nudged Ceilidh. "Besides the fact the people at the high board are obviously talking about me, why does everyone keep looking to the doors?"

Ceilidh let out a long sigh. "The guards from the northern post are returning. After the union between this clan and the Munros, there isn't much need to patrol the border."

"I see," Gisela said. "There seems to be much anticipation." At the high board, the Ross brothers and their uncle, Gregor, didn't seem as preoccupied with the return of the guards.

Just then, Kieran looked to her and met her gaze. A crease formed between his brows and he looked away.

Strange.

Once the meal was over, Gisela decided to go to her small chamber and remain there. In her opinion, it was best to say out of sight until the day she could return home. Hopefully, her mother would send Hamus to check on her cottage and ensure all was well.

Once news spread that she'd left to go marry, scavengers would descend at her home. A shiver of annoyance flowed through her and she pulled her shawl tight.

"Where are ye going?" Kieran was right behind her and the sound of his voice made her suck breath in.

"Ye scared me," Gisela accused, turning around to face him. "I am retiring to my chamber."

"Moira says I should walk ye to the gardens and tell ye about Dun Airgid, our home." His tone was flat and it almost made Gisela laugh.

When a lock of hair fell forward over the side of his face, Gisela fought the urge to sweep it away. "Did ye explain to her that we were not going to be married?"

"Aye, but she insists she knows more than we do. Moira believes herself to have second sight."

"Oh." Gisela wasn't sure what else to add. "If ye insist on a walk, I must fetch a heavier cover." She motioned to the doorway of her bedchamber.

Immediately upon entering the room, the air itself seemed to change. There was a thickness to the atmosphere that made it almost impossible to breathe. The hammering of her heart echoed so loudly, she was sure Kieran heard it.

"Kieran," Gisela began, holding on to the back of a chair to keep steady. "It is a mistake. There is no need for us to…"

He neared, his hazel gaze piercing her. "For us to walk? Talk?" How was it that he remained so calm?

The longer the silence stretched, the harder it became for her to catch her breath. That he could affect her so strongly by just standing in the same room should have been terrifying, but it didn't scare her. Instead, his presence was comforting, almost as if he were a protective shield, keeping her safe from all the wrongs.

It occurred to Gisela that what she wished for most in that moment was to be made love to by Kieran. To belong fully to him for an entire night. Once she returned home, whether she married or not, the memory of one night with the most handsome man she'd ever known would keep her warm inside.

"Stay with me…here…tonight. Show me what it is to make love. I am tired of being dictated to. I wish to do something unreasonable, unthinkable, but something I decide to do."

He remained still, not necessarily in an aloof manner, but more as if he were unsure of what to do first. Gisela slid her hands under his tunic, her palms flat on the warm skin of his sides. With measured movements, she caressed the soft skin, loving the slight tension of every muscle as she touched it.

When he took a sharp breath, it was evident he was enjoying what she did. Thus emboldened, Gisela took the hem of the garment and tugged up until he bent and allowed her to remove it.

His gaze never leaving hers and arms to his sides, there was a silent invitation to continue what she'd started. So she leaned forward and pressed her lips to his chest, kissing it across from one side to the other. When she looked up, his eyes were closed.

Lips curved, she pulled him down and took his mouth.

His tongue pushed past her lips and into her mouth and Gisela raked her fingers through his hair, enjoying the thick locks as they slid between them.

Mouths joined, he unlaced her bodice, impatiently pushing it down off her shoulders. Exposed to him, the first twinge of doubt struck her. But second thoughts were quickly dashed when Kieran's mouth closed over the tip of her left breast.

Moments later, Gisela's clothes pooled at her feet and he led her backwards to the bed, his mouth over hers, hands cupping her bottom, bodies against each other.

Kieran's body was as beautiful as the man, perfectly sculptured, taut skin over well-defined muscles. A light sprinkling of hair across his chest accentuated the broadness.

Lifting her into his arms, Kieran laid her atop the bedding and lowered beside her. With excruciating slowness, he ran his hand down between her breasts to her stomach. Every inch of her skin came to life. Need overtook her until she wanted to scream.

They kissed for a long time while exploring each other's bodies. It was gratifying when he remained still as Gisela ran her hands down his back to his bottom and then explored his chest and ridges of his stomach.

She wasn't sure if it was what people did, but just touching and kissing him was amazing.

What exactly would happen next, Gisela didn't know. But the exploration and kissing were wonderful. If it continued forever, it would not be long enough.

Gisela's breathing hitched when his hand slid further down her body.

"AH!" SHE GASPED when his hand reached between her legs, fingers exploring her sex. It was not an unpleasant feeling, quite the opposite. The sensations were new to her and she wasn't exactly sure what to do.

As if on command, her legs parted and her hips lifted. Every single part of her body reacting to the caresses.

Soon she was writhing, so filled with need that she wanted to cry. "Kieran, please..."

He took her mouth again. The entire time, his index finger circled the secret part of her until Gisela lost all reason and cried out. It was as if the sky opened up and she flew straight up past it to the darkness beyond.

She wasn't sure how long it took before reality began to return but, in that moment, Kieran's fingers began the sweet torture anew, sending her reeling into an abyss of ecstasy.

As she floated, he guided her hand to his staff. It was silky, but thick and she wrapped her fingers around it, stroking the length. He guided her to pleasure him and Gisela couldn't resist. She watched as he became undone, lost in the ministrations. He was so very beautiful with his eyes closed and his lips parted. His body became taut with anticipation until he could no longer hold back and he spilled.

Gisela grabbed his face and brought his mouth to hers. Hungry for more, she lifted up her hips urging for more.

"Ye are perfect," Kieran whispered in her ear. "Allow yerself to release again." Once again, he touched her in just the right way.

Gisela closed her eyes, concentrating on the wonderful sensations, the caresses of his hands over her skin and the continuous movements and his heated kisses.

The floating sensations returned and she grabbed Kieran's shoulders, her fingernails digging into his body, using him as an anchor. Once again, she lost control and let out a hoarse cry.

Tears pricked her eyes at the thought that once the moment was over, once again, they'd return to the distant relationship.

He rolled to his side and held her against him, her head on his shoulder. "I will stay here with ye tonight."

She released a long breath. "Good," Gisela replied.

Cupping her jaw, he tipped her face up to his. She'd never seen him so relaxed, at ease. He studied her. "I meant what I said.

Ye are perfect."

Gisela shrugged. "Do not be thinking that what just happened gives ye any rights over me."

"I would be disappointed if ye didn't say that."

Unable to keep from it, she kissed him and he returned the kiss. This time, it was sweet and slow. "I do not expect anything from ye, Kieran Ross."

He seemed to ponder her words. "Moira will be disappointed."

Not him. Gisela pushed the thought away. After all, there were probably countless women who'd wished he be with them this night. She doubted she was his first virgin. Although it was on the tip of her tongue, she didn't ask.

"As soon as the guards return, we leave. If they do not bring news, then Ethan McLeod is in hiding."

"When do the guards return?" Gisela asked, hoping she'd have time to prepare herself for never seeing him again.

"In a day or two."

"A day or two," she repeated. Her chest constricted, confirming that, in her heart, she had been hoping he would ask her to stay.

It would be best to follow her mother's advice and seek a husband once she arrived back on Munro lands. Now that she'd given herself to Kieran, she knew it would be impossible to remain alone. And even though another man would never compare, it would be better than waiting for Kieran who would never come.

CHAPTER FIFTEEN

"WHERE IS GISELA?" Kieran asked Moira the next day. The guards had returned that afternoon, so they would leave the following morning.

In a way, he'd hoped Gisela would have asked to remain there. But more than once, she'd made it abundantly clear it was her desire to return home. The night before had been like no other. He desired her more than any other woman. As much as he wished to, he could not take her virginity, not without marrying her.

He wondered if she'd understood that she remained un-claimed? Gisela was passionate and he'd almost lost control several times. Not claiming her had been one of the hardest things he'd ever done. But the memory of her undone by his hand was something he'd never forget. Never wished to forget.

The minx had been brave asking him to stay with her. At the same time, it was probably because of his looks that she'd wanted to be with him and nothing to do with any feelings between them.

"The flower field."

"Alone?"

Moira studied him. "Nay. Ceilidh is with her. They call up to the guards and are watched. Tis safe enough."

He stalked out and rounded the house, going through a side gate to the field. Immediately, he spotted Gisela. As Moira had said, she was accompanied by Ceilidh.

At nearing, the other woman walked a few feet away to give them privacy. Gisela's gaze met his and her lips curved. Immediately, the picture of what they had done the night before formed and he pushed it away.

"The guards arrived."

"Aye, I saw," she replied, her smile disappearing. "When do we leave?"

"At dawn."

She nodded. "Very well. I will be ready."

Nothing could be said that mattered in that moment, so he turned and walked away.

"He makes me nervous," the woman, Ceilidh, said.

Gisela chuckled. "He is not so bad."

Kieran almost smiled.

THE FAMILIAR CLANG of sword hitting sword rang loud as the guardsmen sparred. Kieran was matched with Tristan that day. His brother was a fierce contender. Strong as an ox, the man often surprised his opponents with his fluidity and speed.

When Kieran barely missed blocking a strike, he glared at his brother. "Are ye trying to kill me?"

Tristan expression was stern. "Yer mind is elsewhere. Are ye already gone from here to track Ethan? Tis dangerous if ye cannot control yer thoughts."

Instead of replying, he turned and thrust forward with his sword. Tristan effectively blocked it. "Ye're becoming predictable." Tristan flung Kieran's arm away and sliced through the air, a move that often caught his opponents off guard.

Although Kieran was able to block the strike, he stumbled back a couple of steps. Angered at his lack of ability, he growled and swung, aiming for Tristan's side.

His brother easily evaded the blow, jumping sideways. He swept a foot across that tripped Kieran, sending him down onto the ground hard. Then as fast as a lightning, Tristan pushed a huge knee into Kieran's shoulder and pressed the hilt of his sword into Kieran's neck.

Even though he wouldn't be cut, Kieran didn't move. Instead, he glared at Tristan. "What are ye doing?"

"Pointing out that ye should not be out there fighting right now. Ye need to wait and travel with at least four guards. Even if Ethan is out there waiting for ye, he can catch ye by surprise. Ye are being hunted, Brother...do not forget that."

"Neither of us has the upper hand in this," Kieran gritted out. His shoulder was throbbing and he was about to attempt to get up when Tristan lifted up and then grabbed Kieran's hand, lifting him off the ground.

"Ye have no idea where he is. Tis a vast area out there."

It was true; the guards had brought no reports of anyone seeing the bastard anywhere. The McLeod lands were northeast of his lands, so taking Gisela home, it would be a good enough route to take.

"I won't rest until I find him. We cannot stop until he is dead." He looked into Tristan's eyes to see that his brother agreed. "Ye know it as well as I do."

"We will send another set of scouts to hunt for him. I promise."

Kieran nodded. Either he'd find Ethan himself this trip or upon his return, he'd find a report from scouts. But not doing something was not an option.

Just as he went to leave, Tristan placed a hand on his shoulder. "Killing Ethan McLeod will not stop the pain."

"I tire of hearing it. I do not feel pain. I feel the need to avenge." So angry that he had to explain it to Tristan, he rounded his brother and stalked away.

Why did everyone say the same thing? Of course it would not end the pain, the loss, but he would feel better about having failed his father.

Suddenly, he grew tired. He searched the courtyard for Gisela, but she wasn't about. In all probability, she had gone to see about preparing to return home.

The air stilled, as if in anticipation, waiting for an elusive answer that would release it to once again flow. That was his life. It was stilled.

There would be no moving forward, no new beginnings for him. Once he found Ethan McLeod and killed him, only then would Kieran consider a future.

The strong possibility he'd die was not something that would deter him. As a matter of fact, dying before killing Ethan first was the only thing he feared.

ALTHOUGH NOT HUNGRY and uneasy, Kieran attended last meal. He sat next to his uncle, Gregor, who was unusually somber. It suited Kieran perfectly as he wasn't in the mood to make unnecessary conversation.

"It will never be the same," his uncle said, not explaining what he meant.

Instinctively, he knew it was about his father. During the spring season, his father and uncle often went hunting together and spent many days out in the forest. He studied his uncle's profile. It ached to look upon him because of the resemblance to his father.

"Ye're right."

"And yet, life continues. Soon, Malcolm will have a son or daughter, Tristan as well. And ye will one day fall in love and begin a family. Tis what life is about."

Not wishing to disrespect his uncle, he remained quiet. Scanning the room, Gisela's absence was notable. She was not with Ceilidh at a nearby table. Was she preparing for their trip? It wasn't as if there was much for her to pack.

Deciding to check in on her, he stood and went to her bedchamber.

The door was slightly ajar, so he knocked. When there was no reply, he opened it and peered inside. There was nothing amiss, but Gisela was not there. Her few belongings had not been packed.

After inspecting the rest of the house and then the courtyard and garden, he wondered if she'd gone to the stables.

He noticed three guards standing at the gate talking. One man held a woman's shoe. His heartbeat sped up as he walked closer.

"Where did ye find it?"

"I just came from hunting in the forest and found this near the edge."

Another guard piped up, "A woman seems to have lost her shoe."

He motioned for two other guards to come to him. "Go through the entire keep and find Gisela Munro. The lass who came with Tristan from Munro lands."

One guard's mouth fell open. "Yer betrothed?"

He didn't wish to argue. "Aye. Find her."

Long moments later, it was determined Gisela was gone. Something had happened to her. She'd not run off, not without her belongings and then losing a shoe. Someone had taken her.

It was much later that Kieran and the guards returned from scouring the surrounding areas. Exhausted from riding for hours, Kieran trudged into the house.

Too exhausted to think about what he'd do the next day, he walked into the great room to find only his uncle still up. He was sitting in front of the hearth with the hounds at his feet.

"Any news?" he asked, already knowing the answer by the lack of enthusiasm in Gregor's face.

"Nay. A second set of guards has gone to search for the lass. I am up only because the hounds woke me." His uncle looked from the fire in the hearth to him. "Rest, Kieran. Not much can be done until morning."

He lowered to a chair next to his uncle's. "Why would anyone wish to harm her?"

"Have ye considered that perhaps a lover left behind came for her?"

The thought had merit and yet he knew for a fact that Gisela had not been enamored with anyone. She'd fought too hard not to be tied down. However, it didn't mean she'd not left someone behind who held out hope of being with her.

"Could be."

There was a serenity to his uncle that he sometimes envied. At the same time, Kieran couldn't understand how he could be so calm when knowing his only brother's killer was out there, alive and well.

As if guessing his thoughts, Gregor met his gaze. "Ye will leave in the morning and continue on yer quest to avenge Robert's death."

Kieran nodded. "I cannot rest until the bastard is dead."

His uncle let out a long breath. "He was so very proud of all three of ye, but often told me ye reminded him most of himself when he was young."

Although his father was a strong laird, Kieran didn't consider him to be the vengeful type. "How?"

"When yer father was young, before marriage, he was abrasive and rash. It often caused him to make the wrong decisions."

"What changed?"

Gregor's lips curved. "A lass. Her name was Aurora. She was the love of his life. I do not mean to disrespect yer mother. But yer father and mother's marriage was arranged, as ye well know." His uncle took a breath. "Robert planned to give up everything to be with Aurora, but she did not want him to lose the lairdship for her. So she married another to keep him from it."

"So she did not love my father as much as he did her."

Gregor shook his head. "On the contrary, she loved him so much that she married a man without love to keep yer father from losing his birthright."

Kieran scowled. "And he did not resent her for it?"

"At first, aye. However, they loved each other too much and continued to be friends until she and her husband left here to live with his family in the south."

The hounds' heads came up as four guards walked in. Once spotting Kieran and Gregor, they neared.

"We went north. A farmer told us he saw a man riding with a woman. Although he was a bit far away, by the description, it could be Ethan McLeod."

Kieran jumped to his feet. "Where? What direction was he going?"

"He was near Kildonan and heading northwest."

"Ye should not go until dawn," his uncle stated.

But Kieran was already heading to the door, sword in hand.

CHAPTER SIXTEEN

CEILIDH RUSHED THROUGH the great room and then past the kitchen to the courtyard. She'd just heard the news of Gisela missing and wished to find Ian. A group of guards had left that morning to help search for her, but surely more would be sent. Gisela was in grave danger. Ethan McLeod was mad and didn't hesitate to kill.

Just as she exited the house, she ran straight into Ruari and stumbled backward. "Where are ye going in such a rush?" he grumbled.

Instantly, her cheeks reddened. "To find Ian. I hope to get news about Gisela."

"Nothing new. Ian went with the group to search for her." He gave her a stern look. "Ye should go back inside."

It was then she noticed a group of men lined up. None looked happy and by the looks of it, didn't appreciate her presence.

"What is going on out there?" Ceilidh craned her neck to look around Ruari.

He remained silent and motioned to the doorway. "Go back inside."

Given no choice, she plodded back inside and then went right to enter the kitchen.

Moira, along with several maids, stood at the window, peering out.

"Ruari wouldn't allow me outside," Ceilidh said and hurried to squeeze between them.

"They are going to be punished," Moira replied. "They were on guard last night and I will venture to say that whoever took Gisela was able to get onto the keep grounds."

"Oh, no." Ceilidh clutched her hands together and watched as the laird stalked back and forth.

Laird Ross shouted at one of the guards, "Where were ye posted?"

The guard replied and Laird Ross moved to the next man in line.

As each man replied, some were questioned again.

"How could this have happened?" Ceilidh asked. "Every time I have come here, I have always been encountered by a guard. This is horrible."

"Aye, it is. However, they must never become so comfortable that something like this happens. Those who mean harm are wily creatures." Moira turned away from the window. "Come along, ladies. We must ensure first meal is prepared."

"What will happen to them?" Ceilidh remained at the window. "Will they be whipped?"

Moira gave her a stern look. "Tis not our concern. It has not happened in a very long time. It will be the first time Laird Malcolm is faced with something like this."

Just then, Elspeth walked in, hands atop her stomach. She'd developed the habit since her pregnancy began to show. One day she had a flat stomach and it seemed that overnight it swelled to a soft mound. She let out a sigh. "Any news?"

"Come sit, my lady." Moira hurried to her and attempted to pull her to a chair. Elspeth held out her hands to stop the cook. "I sit too much already." She neared the window where Ceilidh had remained.

"This is horrible." She frowned. "If not because Malcolm

warned me against it, I would go out there and give those men a good lecture."

"I do believe they will receive more than that," Moira replied, once again joining them at the window.

After a few minutes, Gregor walked in from the courtyard and past the kitchen. Ceilidh hurried to catch up with him. "What will happen to the men?"

"All eight will be given five lashes and they will be restricted to their quarters when not on guard." He made an annoyed gesture, throwing his hands up. "If it were up to me, all of them would be given ten lashes and the leaders would receive more."

When Ceilidh made her way back to the kitchen, one of the maids was crying. Obviously, a guard who was about to be lashed was important to her.

With a bowl in each hand, Elspeth motioned for her to come to the table. "We must mix some poultice. The men will require healing after this."

"I think men should not be beaten. Although they were at fault, a reprimand and restriction would be enough punishment." Ceilidh sighed and patted the crying maid's shoulder. "Is one of them yer love?"

"Nay, my brother," the maid replied and began sobbing. "He was assigned to the ramparts. He should not be punished as much."

Moira placed a cup of hot liquid in front of the maid. "Herbs to calm ye down. Come now," she motioned to the others. "Let us finish cooking."

By the time first meal was prepared and everyone ate, it was late.

Most of the guards refused treatment, which annoyed Elspeth. They treated only three, all very young and unused to corporal punishment.

"Barbaric," Ceilidh said as she rinsed her hands. "Elspeth, ye should have interceded."

Her friend nodded. "Aye, if I had known. I did not expect

this." She wiped a tear. "I worry for Gisela. What she may be enduring."

"If she is alive." Ceilidh said out loud what they'd both been thinking.

"Poor girl."

They made their way back to the house, stopping upon finding a guard who'd been lashed and stood by a well, pulling up a bucket and then pouring the water over himself to wash the blood away.

"Ye should let me put something on that. It will heal faster," Elspeth said, placing her wooden healing box on the well's wall. "Sit and I will see to it."

The man grumbled under his breath, but sat down. His back was reddened, the skin broken in several places. Angry slashes crisscrossed not only his back, but the backs of his arms as well.

Both Ceilidh and Elspeth made quick work of applying the poultice and then wrapped a bandage around one of his arms where a cut was particularly deep.

The man thanked them and walked toward the guard quarters to begin the other part of his punishment.

"They will only be feed water and pottage," a lead guard said as he walked by. He gave them a warning look. "Nothing else."

Elspeth placed her hands on both hips. "We will hope they will not be required to defend our home, because they will be too weak."

The man didn't reply. Instead, he continued on toward the guard quarters.

"This is ridiculous," Elspeth said, hurrying toward the house. Ceilidh had to practically run to keep up with her.

"Wh-where are ye going?" Ceilidh asked, trying to keep up.

"To speak to Malcolm. The men have been whipped and will be on restriction. They will eat what everyone else does."

CHAPTER SEVENTEEN

Ethan

I F HE WERE inclined to seduce a woman, it would definitely be one like the rebellious woman who stared him down. Even tied to a tree, she emanated defiance and lack of fear. It was a front, of course, by the slight tremble to her bottom lip. But nonetheless, she was formidable.

Ethan spit on the ground, his saliva mixed with blood. The insolent wench had head-butted him when he'd neared to try to give her a drink. Ethan studied her for a moment longer.

He had to admit, of all the brothers, Kieran had chosen the best woman. Now it would be his pleasure to, once again, cause him great pain. Kieran Ross would be present to witness the death of his beautiful love. It would serve him right. It would serve everyone right for underestimating him.

"Ye are the man who came to my cottage. What do ye want with me?" she asked once again. This time, her voice was low. She had to be exhausted. They'd traveled all night and late into the morning without stopping. It was only out of care that his mount could falter that Ethan stopped.

He knew precisely where he'd go. And he would leave a trail

of markers.

And of course, the idiot would follow. Even if not out of love for the woman, Kieran would come because he thought himself the hunter, the one in pursuit.

It was a warmer day than usual, not one cloud to shade the sun from beaming down. Thankfully, he'd spotted a shallow creek so his mount could have its fill. The wench had to be thirsty, but it didn't matter now. She'd sealed her fate. From this point on, she'd not be given anything to drink or eat.

Ethan walked in a circle, searching the surroundings, ensuring no one was close. Not yet. His destination was perfect and he had to reach it before Kieran caught up to them.

His lips curved.

No one was greater at setting traps, better at manipulating people to do his will. It was time everyone, including his family, realized how intelligent he was.

They thought him mad. Although not saying it out loud, the way they'd looked at him, especially his father, made it obvious. They had betrayed him, thrown him into a room in the bowels of the keep and locked the door.

To keep him out of harm from the Ross' they'd claimed. But it wasn't true. They, along with everyone else, were aware of his power and feared how many would die as he wielded it and became the new laird of Clan Ross. Idiots.

They'd sealed their fates as well. His own family would fall beneath the heel of his boot.

Not only would he conquer all the Ross' lands, but also the McLeod's. He just needed time. Which would come once he rid himself of Kieran. The man was relentless in pursuing him. Once dead, the other two brothers would be easy to dispose of. In their grief, they'd become careless and distracted.

"I asked ye a question." Kieran's woman came into focus and Ethan loomed over her.

"I am Ethan McLeod. The most powerful man ye will ever meet. Tis a shame, really, that ye will die before having the opportunity to recount about me."

He considered for a moment that perhaps it would be a good idea to bring a young lad along with him on his travels. Then send him into villages to tell of his conquests.

All in good time.

"Ye are a fool is what ye are. No one will come for me." The beauty looked directly into his eyes. He almost looked away, but caught himself. She was a pawn, not someone who should affect him in any way. Certainly not make him feel less than who he was.

"We leave soon. Prepare yerself." He turned away.

She let out an indignant huff. "Exactly what do ye expect me to do? Peer in the looking glass and sort out my hair?"

He stalked to her, grabbed the hem of her dress and tore a strip. He then went to a thorny bush and pulled the piece of cloth along the brambles until it caught. It would look as if she'd hurried past. It would leave a clue for whoever followed them. By the time Kieran stumbled upon them, his trap would be set.

Considering she'd not hesitate to bite or kick, Ethan rounded the thin tree and untied her. Then he yanked her up from behind and guided her between two bushes.

"Relieve yerself and ye can wash at the creek. Do not try to escape." He then untied her hands and stepped back.

He waited until she neared the creek's edge and bent over to wash and drink. Then as quick as a striking snake, he placed his hand on the back of her head and pushed her face under the water.

The woman fought. She became frantic, kicking and scratching. The water sloshed as he struggled to keep her head submerged. Finally, as she began to slow, he released her and yanked her back.

Sputtering and coughing horribly, she lay on the ground flopping about like a fish. He didn't feel anything other than curiosity as she sat up, still choking on the water she'd inhaled. The woman's face became alarmingly red as she gasped for air.

She was a sight, hair plastered to the sides of her head and dress muddy and wet.

"Do ye see now? Ye are mine to do with as I wish. It will not be long before Kieran Ross follows."

He watched as she struggled to get a good breath. Needing a closer look at his handiwork, Ethan loomed over her.

"Tis a shame, really. I would think someone of yer beauty would be more interested in a man like me."

The woman had the audacity to glare. If he had any reservations about killing her, they'd be dashed by her impertinence. Grabbing her by the hair, he dragged her back to the water.

She fought, but was too weak to protest. Stupid woman, he was much too strong for her.

Once again, he dunked her head into the water. Her flailing only added to the enjoyment. If only he could hold her down until her life ebbed. But no, it was much too easy and too soon. Ethan lifted her head and, this time, she barely sputtered.

Finally after a few moments, her entire body was racked with coughs and she whimpered and tried in vain to drag herself away from him.

"Ye see now how easy it would be for me to end yer life? I will kill ye soon, but not until he can watch."

Ethan yanked her to her feet. She faltered, barely able to stand. There was no need to attempt any type of care, so he shoved her forward toward the horse. She fell to the ground and, once again, he pulled her up to stand. The coughing was lessening somewhat, which was a shame, really. When she tripped and fell, the woman began to cry.

A chuckle escaped Ethan.

The power he had over people was intoxicating.

FOR INTERMINABLE HOURS, Gisela either fell asleep or blacked out.

The never-ending hours of riding wore on her. Not only was she still in shock from almost drowning, but she was also wet, cold, muddy and hungry.

It had been a long while since they'd stopped and even longer since her captor deemed to give her a drink or a bite of food. He was saving it for himself, she mused. Since she wouldn't live long, there was no need for nourishment of any kind.

"Water?" The word came out as a whisper.

Her request was ignored. Too tired to care, Gisela began to cry. Darting out her tongue, she tasted the salty tears and slumped forward. At first during the ride, she'd tried to reason with the man. She had told him Kieran would not come for her. But he'd known Kieran would follow. Even if not for her, Kieran would come for him.

Once again, blackness threatened. It could be she would die before Kieran reached her. Too weak to remain awake, Gisela gave in, not wanting to fight what was inevitable.

The next time she came to, it was dark. Gisela did her best to get comfortable, but her entire body shook from the chill of the night and her wet clothing. Although the man had made a fire, she couldn't get warm. He'd placed her just a bit too far from the fire so the heat didn't quite reach her.

It was a horrible way to spend her last days, Gisela thought. Hungry and cold with no one offering comfort was a miserable existence. When tears spilled, she marveled that she could still cry.

Unlike her, her captor seemed at ease. His back to the cave wall, he snored softly. She eyed him for a moment and then looked around.

With hands and feet bound, there was little she could do to get away. They were in a small cave, the entrance blocked by the slumbering man.

If she managed to get past him, she would have to get past the branches he'd piled at the entryway to keep the wind out. The noise would wake him.

Gisela closed her eyes and pictured Kieran. What was he doing at the moment? In all probability, he was searching for them. If he did find them, Ethan McLeod would immediately kill her. For whatever reason, the man hated Kieran and would do anything to hurt him.

The joke was on him because although Kieran and she had become close, it was doubtful her death would hurt him.

If anything, it would be a good distraction to help Kieran finally get the upper hand on his enemy.

She shivered and wiggled closer to the fire. If only time could be turned back. Instead of shaking from the cold in a cave, she would be back in her little cabin in the woods. She'd be in that quiet place with only herbs and, on occasion, her brother and mother to keep her company.

In her gut, Gisela knew she'd never return to the cabin. Her life, although simple and insignificant, had been a good one. Upon receiving news of her demise, her mother would grieve for a short period. Her brother would take it harder. In all probability, Ethan would be dead by the time they got the news. So thankfully, her brother would not be faced with the decision to head out on a quest for justice.

Ethan McLeod would die soon. There was little doubt in her mind that Kieran was the stronger of the two and would have his vengeance.

Either way, she'd not know how it would all end, as the man who sat mere feet from her would be her killer.

"WAKE UP!" A kick to her leg startled Gisela awake. Somehow, she'd survived the night. Although she was still weak from lack of food and shivering all night, at least her dirty clothes were somewhat dry.

"We leave immediately."

She peered to the cave's entrance. It was dim outside but would be dawn soon as the first signs of sunrays arrived.

Before she could stand, he dragged her up and toward the

entrance. "I do not have time to waste with ye. Perhaps I should leave ye along the way as a marker for him to follow."

When he laughed, a shiver traveled up Gisela's spine. Was it her time to die?

"Are ye sure he would follow ye right after? Or will ye be forced to spend many more nights looking over yer shoulder?" Her voice was weak, but she managed to speak loudly.

Instead of a reply, he tied a binding around her face to shield her eyes and then bound her hands. When he shoved her forward, Gisela stumbled. If Kieran did not kill the horrible man, she would.

By the time they mounted and continued on their way, she could hear a bird's song. Morning had arrived. It was impossible to tell in which direction they rode. She did her best to keep an ear out for sounds that would give some sort of clue, but it was useless. The clop-clop of the horse's hooves and the wind through leaves were all she could make out. The man breathed evenly, seeming at ease holding her atop the horse.

Unlike when she'd ridden with Kieran, this man managed to keep a distance between them, ensuring she leaned forward at the waist. It was tiring, but she didn't mind as she'd rather not have more contact with him than needed.

Abruptly, he pulled the horse to a stop and then they veered to the side. Just as she was about to say something, he slapped a hand over her mouth.

"Keep quiet."

The sounds of a wagon being pulled reached her ears and Gisela hoped they'd be spotted. She racked her brain for what to do to get attention, but nothing came to mind. With her hands bound and unable to make noise, she could only remain still as the cart and rider continued by them.

Ethan let out a long breath. "There are too many people on this road. I must find another. Although it will take another night…" He seemed to realize he spoke out loud and abruptly stopped speaking. With a low growl, he guided the house back onto the road.

"Where are we going?" Gisela's voice sounded more like a croak than anything else.

"I suppose there is no harm in telling ye, since it will be yer resting place. We head to Morgan's Peak."

The name meant nothing to Gisela.

When they stopped again, Gisela was barely able to totter to behind a group of leafy bushes to relieve herself. Her legs trembled when she crouched down, making it difficult to retain her balance.

There had to be a way to escape. From the many times Ethan had been yawning, he was exhausted. Not anxious to be bound, she lingered in the bushes.

Feeding the horse and guiding it to a tiny trickle of a stream, he didn't watch her. It was obvious he considered her too weak to get far if she decided to run.

The wind blew warm across her face and Gisela studied the surroundings. The trees were not dense, but there seemed to be a path by them. Hopefully, it meant there was a village nearby.

At first, she walked a bit away, pretended to search for something to eat. Then upon determining she was just far enough away, she picked up her skirts and sprinted toward the trees.

Her chest ached as she continued to run. It was only through sheer willpower that she continued running. Low branches whisked past Gisela's arms and face. Several times, her hair became caught in the limbs.

It had been a few minutes since she'd heard him coming after her and she slowed, unable to keep the fast pace. Frantic, she looked around, unable to make any sense of what direction she was headed. There were no longer signs of a path because, in the panic of escaping, she'd lost sight of it.

There was rustling behind her and she dove to the ground to hide behind a fallen tree.

A trio of deer came into view, their heads turning in every direction, always alert. Not stopping, they continued on past her, then suddenly sprinted away.

Gisela almost smiled. If she went the direction the deer had come from, it could be safe.

Her legs barely sustained her upright when she straightened and her stomach grumbled, demanding food.

"Soon," she whispered, a promise with little basis. She took a step forward and immediately realized her mistake. The deer had been frightened and darted away because they'd sensed someone coming.

The hard slap sent her sideways and she didn't bother crying out. When Ethan pulled her up by the hair, she bit back a scream.

CHAPTER EIGHTEEN

"**A**NY NEWS?" CEILIDH hurried to Ian who walked into the great room. His expression was unreadable, the flatness in his eyes not exposing his thoughts. Whenever he worked, her betrothed transformed from the caring, soft-spoken man to a menacing warrior.

"Ye may come with me as I speak to the laird," he said and continued straight to the high board where Elspeth and Malcolm sat listening to clanspeople's concerns.

As soon as Ian walked up, Malcolm waved the group who'd been speaking to move back. He glanced at Ceilidh, but didn't send her away.

"Speak," he commanded.

Ian nodded in deference. "There were reported sightings. Most informed us that the woman, Gisela, was taken north toward Morgan's Peak."

The men exchanged a look Ceilidh couldn't decipher and then Malcolm spoke. "Did ye send men there?"

"Aye, ten."

"That should be enough."

"No, send more, Malcolm." Elspeth grabbed his arm. "Yer brother goes alone and we do not know how he will react if something has befallen Gisela. Ye should send more men."

"Tis only one woman and one man. There is no need for a large contingent…"

Elspeth's nostrils flared and she pinned her husband with a narrowed glare. "She is a Munro. Our clans are united now. Ye cannot allow for anything bad to happen to her."

Her words had obviously sunk in because the laird nodded. "Ye are right."

Malcolm looked to Ian. "Did the rest return with ye?"

"Only half, the rest remained a day's ride away in case they are needed." Ian motioned with his head for two men to come near. "What message would ye like to send?"

"Order them to Morgan's Peak. Send a messenger to find Tristan and inform him of the situation. He will decide what to do."

"I will return to my men," Ian said.

Elspeth smiled at Ian. "Be with care and bring her and Kieran back alive."

It was obvious that Elspeth was the perfect wife to the laird. Although Ceilidh had often wondered how she'd tamed the hard man, it was obvious he doted upon her and took her advice on matters.

With a slight bow, Ian turned and stalked away. Ceilidh had to run to keep up with his long strides.

"Ian…"

"Come." Ian took her hand and led her down a corridor to his room. "We do not have much time."

"Do ye need me to get anything for yer trip back?"

"Nay," he replied, wrapping his arm around her waist and then guiding her to his narrow bed. "Just allow me to have ye."

Moments later, he lay beside her, chest heaving and Ceilidh reached across and ran her hand down his chest. "I am visiting Kildonan in the next day or so. Do ye think it safe to travel?"

Lifting his head, he studied her face. "Take guards with ye."

"I do not have that privilege. I am but a companion."

"Invite Elspeth then."

Ceilidh kissed his jawline and sat up. "She is with child and Malcolm does not allow her to travel. I will ask Ruari if the young stable lad who also has family there can go with me."

When Ian stood, she helped him fasten his breeches and they walked out of the room together. He pulled her close and kissed her once again.

"Wait until I return. I can take ye."

She bit her bottom lip. "If ye do not return in four days, I will ask Elspeth to get me an escort. But I really must see my family."

Ceilidh could tell Ian was torn. It wasn't that she wished to defy him, but more to set some ground rules. She was not the kind of woman to be ordered about or to be constantly protected. All her life, she'd been independent. That wasn't about to change because of marriage.

She walked with him as he headed out to the courtyard where his mount and several guards waited. Within minutes, he would be mounted and gone. It was preferable not to watch his departure, so she headed inside the kitchens to find Moira.

The woman beamed upon spotting her. The warm smile made Ceilidh glad to have gained such a wonderful second mother in Ian's.

"Did he leave already?" Moira asked as she stirred a large pot. "I would have thought he would have volunteered to remain."

"It's not in his nature," Ceilidh said, peering into the pot. "I had hoped he would. We've yet to discuss any wedding details."

Laughter rang loudly from both Moira and another of the kitchen maids. Finally, Moira was able to calm enough to speak. "Darling girl, men care little of what it takes to plan a wedding. All they care about is the wedding night."

Wide-eyed, Ceilidh felt her face heat. Did Moira think her a virgin?

Moira gave her a knowing look and turned to one of her helpers. "They were too impatient. They didn't wait, did they?"

Ceilidh's eyes rounded and her cheeks burned hot.

"Nay. I've seen him sneak out of her room in the wee hours," a maid replied, sending everyone back to hysterical laughter.

"And she out of his," another piped up.

While everyone laughed, Ceilidh pressed her lips together, doing her best not to tell them to mind their own business. However, a few moments later, she was having a difficult time not joining in.

"I do think it is rude to spy on people," she finally said with as much indignity as she could muster.

"Oh, girls, don't be upset." She then smiled. "However, I am sure he will be looking forward to me and he remaining in the same bed all night."

Chuckling, Moira shook her head. "Besides, ye're both horrible at keeping secrets. Like now," Moira pointed at Ceilidh. "Yer laces are half-undone."

Slowly, she looked down to her chest. It was true, the laces were loose, leaving her breasts half-exposed. Before she could think of something to say, blonde curls fell from pins and cascaded over her face.

This time, she had to join in when the maids dissolved into loud guffaws.

IAN RETURNED LATE that night. His horse had a limp, keeping him from continuing with the rest of the guards.

He was grumpy and tired after a day of hard riding and sat in a chair in front of the hearth with a tankard of ale on a table at his elbow. He managed to brighten upon Ceilidh nearing, his clear gaze following her every move. Never had any man made her feel so alive, so alluring. It was as if with Ian, a new Ceilidh had been born.

She lowered to a chair next to his.

"Ye have questions?" he asked, meeting her gaze.

Ceilidh bit her bottom lip. "It hardly seems the appropriate time, but I have to visit mother and require an escort."

"Yer visit can wait until I can take ye. Right now, I cannot." His stern reply was so unlike him that her eyes rounded and her mouth fell open.

"What do ye mean? I know there is much to be done, but our wedding is something that cannot be put off for long."

He softened somewhat, but Ceilidh could tell his mind was on what his men were doing and the matter of Gisela. She understood. However, what if she came to be with child? She'd not shame her family.

Was this to be her life? That everything, including their own wedding, came far behind his tasks as guard to Laird Ross?

She gave him a long look. "With or without ye, I will travel to the village. And," she paused, sinking her pointer finger into his hard chest. "We will be married before fall."

Ceilidh raced away, not wishing the tears that spilled to ruin the façade that she'd portrayed.

"Stop," Elspeth called from behind Ceilidh. "Where are ye going?" Her friend walked closer, barely able to catch her breath.

"Ye are getting quite large. I wonder if there aren't two," Ceilidh teased, wiping at her tears. The last thing she wanted to do was worry her friend who, despite everything, remained strong.

"Walk me to my chambers," Elspeth said with a sigh. "I grow tired early these days and it is quite bothersome."

"That is because ye try to be everywhere at once and maintain the busy schedule of a laird's wife. Ye have to rest," Ceilidh scolded as she took her friend's elbow and walked down the corridor toward the last door.

"Ceilidh," Ian said, coming up behind them.

Elspeth turned and looked up at the tall warrior. "If ye do not keep my friend happy, I will ensure she finds a man who will."

She slid a look to Ceilidh. "What do ye require? Why were ye upset?"

"I wish to visit Mum and asked for an escort to Kildonan."

Her friend turned to Ian. "Ensure four guards are set to escort Ceilidh to Kildonan, remain two nights and bring her back." Once again, Elspeth's gaze moved to her. "I do not wish for ye to be away much longer than that. I would like ye here with me…in case." She didn't need to explain further to Ceilidh. Elspeth had been overly sensitive since becoming pregnant.

Ian lowered his head just a bit in acquiescence. "Of course, Lady Ross."

"And see that they bring my mother back." Elspeth waved a hand. "Go now. I require private time with Ceilidh."

With a furrow between his brows, he looked to Ceilidh. "I will escort ye."

Ceilidh shrugged. "It is not required."

Upon Ian turning and walking away, he gave a low growl.

Elspeth slapped both hands over her mouth and hurried into the chamber. Once the door closed, she chuckled. "He is quite angry, wouldn't ye say?"

"Oh, he is," Ceilidh replied, unable to keep from frowning. She'd not meant for Ian to be directed by the laird's wife. It had just happened.

"Tomorrow during the travel to Kildonan, ye will have plenty of time to talk and set things straight. Ensure ye are always truthful and explain how ye feel without making him feel as if ye're placing blame."

Ceilidh studied her friend. "Ye have always been so strong and intelligent. As if ye were meant to be Laird Ross' wife."

IN THE KITCHEN, Ian's mother sat at the table, her feet up on a stool and a cup of warm cider in her hand. As part of her routine, Moira enjoyed quiet time alone in the evenings while sitting in front of a cheery fire.

When Ian entered, she motioned to a small pot next to the hearth. "Pour a cup and join me, Son."

"Women are complicated creatures," he said upon sitting. "I never know if Ceilidh is happy or…" he circled his hand in the air, not sure what word to use. "She wishes to go to Kildonan even now when the other woman was stolen away."

Moira gave a soft chuckle. "Life is hard, dear one. There is always something horrible happening in a large clan like this one. If ye wait for all to settle, yer marriage will never take place."

"I am certain that I wish to marry Ceilidh and have her as my wife." He gave up and looked into the fire. "Some days, I wonder if it will be a mistake."

Moira's expression remained calm, as if she didn't have a care in the world at the moment. Ian loved the woman with all his heart and knew his mother felt the same. In that, he had never had any kind of uncertainty.

However, when it came to Ceilidh, he always felt as if it were too good to be true. His chest ached each time her expression became pensive or solemn. "Is it common to have doubts?"

His mother chuckled. "Aye, it is."

Scowling into his cup, Ian stared into the fire. "Ye have always been a good mother to me. Never once did ye complain about the lot life gave ye. When Da died, ye worked harder to ensure I never wanted for anything. For this, I admire ye most."

Moira's soft smile when she met his gaze made Ian's heart swell.

"Ye will one day be a good father as well. I know ye love me, Son. And I am willing to guess ye feel strongly for Ceilidh and it scares ye, for ye have only known her a short while."

Covering his mother's hand with his, he met her gaze. "I could never love someone more than ye, Mum."

"Don't be silly," Moira said, laughing. She pulled her hand from his and cupped his face.

"Tell me, Son. Can ye picture yer life without the lass?"

He let out a long sigh. "Nay, I cannot."

"There's yer answer then. Marry the girl and be happy. I will always be here for both of ye and any bairns that will soon follow."

Ian chuckled. "Ye'd better be."

⤜⫸✦⫷⤛

ELSPETH WOKE WHEN Malcolm entered their quarters. The bed dipped as he slid under the covers and let out a tired breath. By the time he came to bed lately, her husband was exhausted. Elspeth wasn't sure if he did it on purpose to keep from taking her physically or because there was always so much happening.

Snuggling as close as her protruding stomach would allow, she placed her head on his shoulder. "Is it always like this? So much strife and danger?"

"Nay," he replied and kissed her forehead. "Do not fret."

"I am not fretting," she explained. "I'm just needing to understand. What was it like before the battles between our clan and the McLeod?"

"Peace for long periods. We did have some problems, feuding families, missing people and always a need to guard our borders." He hugged her closer. "With each day that passes, I admire my da more."

"Would ye send people away from the borders if they came with needs? Tried to feed their children?" Elspeth asked. She was about to continue to speak, but stopped when Malcolm shook his head.

"There are ways for them to seek asylum, Elspeth. They should petition the laird for permission. If they truly have a need, they are not turned away or run off our lands. However, most people hide and attempt to settle without permission because they do not wish to swear fealty to our clan."

"I understand."

"And yet ye continue to worry."

"I cannot stop thinking about what is happening. Poor Gisela, out there somewhere, frightened and alone."

Malcolm pulled her closer. "My men are out there, Kieran as well. She will be found."

"Ethan McLeod is an evil, vile man. I do not wish to imagine how he is treating her." A tear trickled down her cheek and she allowed it to fall. "What do ye think will happen?"

"I do not know what to think." He was pensive for a long moment. "It surprised me that Kieran would go after her. But then again, he does have a vendetta that eats at him."

"Ye do not suppose he left so hastily because of Gisela then?"

Malcolm sighed. "I do not know. But it does seem my brother is taken with her. He may not even realize it yet."

Elspeth shuddered. "And for him to find out now, it is horrible. Ethan McLeod will not touch his heart when it comes to taking a life. That poor girl."

"Aye, she may not survive being held captive by him. My hope is that, for Kieran's sake, she is found alive."

Through the window, a lonely bird's song seemed to echo their current mood and Elspeth let out a breath. "I will hold on to the hope that she lives. I cannot imagine how it will affect yer brother otherwise."

"Like ye, I cannot fathom my brother's reaction if Gisela Munro meets her demise. Already, he blames himself for our father's death. No matter what anyone says, he holds to the belief he failed our father."

Malcolm shifted. "If I am to be honest, I, too, have wondered if things would have been different if, instead of Kieran, I would have been there."

Not that it mattered after the fact, however. Elspeth felt sad for Kieran in that his thoughts were probably echoed by both of his brothers. That, indeed, he was partly at fault for their father's death for not being alert enough to stop Ethan McLeod.

"There is no use in placing blame or in pondering different outcomes to what has already happened. Feeling that way can only add to Kieran's burden."

Malcolm nodded and pressed a kiss on her lips. "How fortunate I am to have such an intelligent wife. I do believe ye to be a gift from God."

Her heart melted at his compliment and she let out a long sigh.

Elspeth considered that her aloof brother-in-law was probably crazed with fury at the moment. The last thing Kieran Ross needed was additional reason to be bent on revenge. The man would no doubt lose what little control he had if something happened to Gisela.

"I pray for that poor woman and that God gifts Kieran with her for a wife. She is gentle and kind, but with enough fortitude not to allow him much leave."

"Aye, my brother deserves happiness."

CHAPTER NINETEEN

THE SUN ROSE high in the sky, heating his back. Kieran looked across the wide field, seeing nothing out of the ordinary. Cursing under his breath, he urged Laith forward toward a small slope. From atop the slope, a small village came into view and, past it, hills and valleys, plush and green.

Already, he had made a lethal mistake. In his haste to go after Gisela, he'd left his bow and quiver behind. All he had with him was the broadsword Elspeth's father had made for him and not enough coin to purchase weapons.

"Where are ye?" he asked the wind, his eyes squeezed shut. The wind whispered back, but nothing that made sense. It was a jumble of his fears with just a hint of hope. Kieran shook his head, aware of how mad he was acting in that moment.

He directed the horse to a faster gallop to the village. Once there, he'd make inquiries and hopefully hear something. It was doubtful Ethan would go into any establishment, especially with Gisela in tow. The lass would not be silent and demand rescue.

There were a few people about, everyone turning and watching as he rode past the rustic buildings. When he noticed four men huddled around an entryway, he guided the horse closer. It seemed the men were without means and depended on charity to eat. Bowls were passed out to them and they hurried to a tattered table to eat.

Kieran waited patiently until all the men were gone and neared the doorway. An older woman's sharp gaze swept over him. She shrugged and ladled mutton into a bowl and held it out.

"No, thank ye," Kieran said. But when she shoved it into his hands harder, he held it. In truth, it smelled good and he was hungry.

"May I ask if ye have seen a man who had a woman with him? They would be on horseback."

The woman shook her head. "Nay. No one, but I remain indoors most of the day. I have mouths to feed, with much cooking to do."

She turned to a young lad who sat on a three-legged stool and ate. "Jon, what about it? Have ye seen anyone new about?"

The young lad looked up for the first time, noticing Kieran. He put the bowl down so hard that food plopped out of it. Delighted at the new find, two pups hurried over and gobbled up what was left in the bowl. The woman chuckled and ladled more into the bowl.

Ignoring what had happened, the boy approached Kieran, his shrewd eyes narrowing and a slight lift to the corners of his lips. "Information is not just given," he said, studying Kieran. "What are ye willing to pay for what I know?"

Kieran drank from the bowl and handed it back to the woman. "Thank ye." He pulled two coins from a pocket in his tunic and handed them to the woman who smiled, showing several missing teeth.

He then pulled out two additional coins, which he held just out of the lad's reach. "If I pay ye, it depends on how useful what ye know is."

The boy took his time, acting as if what he had to say needed special formulation. "I don't know anything about a man and a woman, but I do know about two who came into town just this morning. A peddler and an archer."

Moments later, Kieran entered the tavern. There at the bar was a man with a bow and quiver strapped to his back. He didn't recognize the man. However, when the man sensed his regard and met his gaze, it was obvious he was a warrior.

Kieran walked straight to the man who tracked his progress. He motioned a woman over. "Ale," he said and motioned to the man. "Ye?"

The stranger nodded. "I'll have one as well." He then motioned for Kieran to sit. Upon lowering to the chair opposite the man, he ensured to know who surrounded them. The stranger had the more preferable spot, with his back to the wall. Kieran sat with his left side to the wall, not the best, but good enough.

Two tankards were placed in front of them and the stranger took a long draw. "What do ye want?" He asked, eyes flat. "I am not for hire."

"I just need information, tis all."

"About?"

"Have ye seen a man traveling with a woman? They would be traveling north. He is about my age, the woman a bit younger. Dark hair, large eyes."

The man scanned the room, remaining silent as he seemed to consider what to reply. "I traveled from the north. I saw many people traveling. Am I to assume the woman is traveling unwillingly?"

"Aye."

"Then no." He met Kieran's gaze. "Anyone traveling with an unwilling woman will stay away from traveled roads and traverse through the forest. I suggest ye find a good hunting hound to help ye with following a trail."

The man emptied his tankard and held out his hand. "I wish ye luck."

Kieran shook the man's hand. "Thank ye. I am Kieran Ross."

The icy blue gaze met Kieran's. "Asmund Keith."

A Norseman with a Scottish surname, interesting.

Kieran remained in the tavern after the archer left. He was

exhausted, but had to continue. If Gisela was still alive, he had to ensure she remained so.

Soon, Ross guards would come upon the village and he wasn't sure how much good it would do. For some reason, Ethan seemed to always be one step ahead.

How could a madman be so cunning, so good at hiding? As frustrating as his searches had been, this time it was worse. Every passing moment, he could not stop imagining what Gisela was going through. Was she injured, hungry?

Kieran placed payment for the ale on the table and walked out of the tavern, searching up and down until he spotted a peddler's wagon.

"Well, I certainly did not expect to see ye again so soon." The familiar peddler waved upon seeing Kieran. "Are ye seeking to travel with me again?" The old man chuckled, patting his old mule's head. "Do ye see that, Elbert? Mister Ross has come upon us again."

"I do not require travel assistance. Just information."

"Sure, of course. What is it ye need to know?" The man's expectant expression made Kieran soften. It was apparent he was lonely and enjoyed conversation.

"I am in search of a man who stole away with a woman from my lands. She has dark hair…"

The peddler held up both hands. "Ye won't believe this, but I believe I have seen a man with a woman who seemed less than enthusiastic to be brought along."

Kieran's chest constricted. "Where? In what direction did they travel?"

The man pointed with his right hand into the hills. "If I am not mistaken, toward Morgan's Peak. Which doesn't make sense. There is nothing there but bleak, grey, jutting rocks and dangerous cliffs."

Resisting the urge to hurry away, Kieran remained. He had to get as much information as possible. "How long ago did ye see them?"

"Late yesterday."

"How far is Morgan's Peak?"

The man looked to the sky, seeking out the sun. "In the direction of the sun setting, about half a day's ride from here."

Kieran pulled out his purse, which he remembered had few coins in it, and handed the man half of the contents. "Thank ye for this and what ye did before."

"This is too much." The man attempted to give Kieran back some of the coins, but he hurried away, too preoccupied to remain and haggle with the man.

"Be with care," the man called out. "It's a dangerous place."

Laith was tethered next to the small cottage where the woman continued feeding those that stopped by. He asked the woman to tell any guards who happened by that he headed to Morgan's Peak. He handed her an additional coin and hurried to his horse.

Once he was mounted, Kieran urged Laith to a gallop and traveled in the direction the peddler had motioned.

After several hours of riding, Kieran came upon a huge area with rocks jutting from the ground. They looked like fingers emerging out of a grave, reaching for sunlight. He slowed Laith and scanned the surroundings.

The horse picked carefully where to step as he'd been trained, but it meant traveling at an excruciatingly slow pace.

Kieran dismounted and tethered his mount to a low-growing tree and continued his trek on foot. If Ethan had brought Gisela through here, how did they not leave a trace?

He walked with care, steadily forward, while listening intently for sounds of others nearby.

A soft sound made him stop in his tracks. It was a distance away, but sounded very much like someone speaking. Searching the surrounding area, Kieran didn't see anyone. It was hard to see between the incline of the hill and the rocks jutting out. He climbed up to higher ground to see better and hesitated upon hearing voices again.

Step by step to the top of the hill, he kept alert, his entire body tense with apprehension. Where were they? At the sound of murmurs, he stopped and listened, but heard nothing more.

His breathing was labored from the climb, and he took slow breaths in order to hear well. There was little vegetation, making it hard to keep hidden. So as not to be discovered, he lowered and peered around a ragged, large rock.

Just a short distance away, he spotted Ethan and Gisela. His heart stopped and his chest constricted at the sight.

Gisela sat on the ground, head down, her hair a tangled mess covering her face. She was still, not moving, but the fact she remained upright made him delirious with relief.

Ethan paced back and forth, his head swinging around in every direction, ensuring not to be taken by surprise. It would be impossible for Kieran to get any closer without being spotted.

"Are ye here yet, Kieran Ross?" Ethan called out and held up a sword. He took a step closer to Gisela and bent at the waist to speak to her.

Kieran couldn't make out what the idiot said, but she shook her head without speaking.

"Ye are wrong," Ethan said loudly. "He will come because he hopes to stop me from killing ye."

The madman walked to a nearby crest and peered down. "Her fall will be perfect, ye know." Then he called out. "She will not survive."

Ethan stalked back to where Gisela sat and yanked her up by the hair. "Come, lovely. Time to teach him a lesson."

When Gisela let out a scream, it was hoarse, like a frog's croak. She was weak, but fought him, biting and kicking.

Taking advantage of Ethan's distraction, Kieran raced forward, bent at the waist, keeping behind the rocks and bushes as much as possible.

He was almost upon them when Ethan swung around. His lips curved and he held the tip of his sword to Gisela's throat. "That is close enough."

"How do ye plan to keep me from killing ye while pushing

her off the edge?" Kieran asked, his voice flat and without emotion.

For a split second, there was a slight flitter of surprise. But then Ethan narrowed his eyes. "Ye care for the lass and won't allow her to come to harm."

Kieran took a step closer. "Are ye certain?"

This time, Ethan slammed the sword's handle to Gisela's temple and shoved her away.

Kieran rushed forward, his sword slicing the air, his mind one move ahead, but Ethan shifted and blocked.

Once again, Kieran attacked and Ethan, who'd always been a good swordsman, blocked effectively. Once, twice and a third time, Ethan was able to block and swing his sword, the fight even between the two men.

As much as Kieran wished to, he did not bother to glance in Gisela's direction. It was his father's death that he had to avenge. No matter what, he'd not allow any distraction after waiting so long for this moment. From this moment, he would not stop until he killed Ethan.

At hearing a moan, he dared at glance to where Gisela was; even though he had just decided not to have any distractions. She lay on the dirt, her upper body flat, twisted at the hips so her legs faced to one side. Her chest lifted and lowered.

Although it reassured him to see that she was alive, the distraction cost him dearly.

The slice across his chest took his breath away. But the action could be used to his advantage. Kieran took advantage of Ethan's momentary jubilation, and thrust forward, cutting into his opponent's side.

Back and forth, they continued. Kieran advanced in an effort to force Ethan to the crest's edge. But knowing exactly what Kieran was trying to do, Ethan fought back, forcing Kieran backwards.

When Kieran stumbled on a rock, Ethan took advantage. The second cut, on his lower left side, did not hurt as much. Fury rushed through him at allowing the man who killed his father to have the upper hand.

He growled and sprinted forward, not giving Ethan a choice but to retreat.

Swish. Clang. Swish. Clang. The sounds of the blades' sweeping motions, followed by the clang were joined with the scuffling of their boots on the ground and the grunts from their exertions.

"Ye will die today, Kieran Ross," Ethan taunted, "then I will kill each of yer brothers. I cannot be stopped." He hesitated when Kieran managed to slice through his upper leg. It wasn't a deep wound, but enough to catch Ethan by surprise.

"I will toss her over the side of the cliff," Ethan mused, his lips curving into a maniacal grin. "And then ye will go after her. Ye should see her die." The man was too far-gone to care or even notice his injuries. Ethan charged with renewed energy and Kieran fought hard to defend against the attack.

When Ethan's strike sent Kieran's sword flying from his hand, he resorted to evading Ethan's sword falls. Kieran managed to move far enough away to grab a long branch and used it to fend off Ethan's relentless attacks. Eyes wide and unfocused, Ethan looked gleeful as he progressed forward.

"Ye cannot beat me. Do ye now see it? I will always win."

Kieran inched closer to his sword, but Ethan jumped in between him and it. "Tell me, Kieran Ross. What do ye think I should do?" He looked over his shoulder to where Gisela lay. "Should I kill her first?"

Kieran ignored him, using the short respite to gather energy. The cut on his side stung, blood dripped onto the ground.

ETHAN ATTACKED AGAIN. It was halfhearted, but without a sword, Kieran was forced to defend. A crack was followed by the branch breaking in two. Ethan lunged and Kieran tripped backward onto the ground.

His chest constricted at the thought that perhaps Ethan would win. That he would kill him and then Gisela. Sliding a look to where Gisela was, he noted she was no longer there.

"Ye will not win, Ethan. Killing me will not change that ye are mad," he yelled, hoping to keep him from turning around. The longer Gisela had to get away, the better.

The tip of Ethan's sword dug into Kieran's throat and he inched backward. "I won't kill ye, not right now."

He then slid the sword downward, his eyes shining and his lips curved. "Ye have to see her die first."

Kieran cried out and went rigid when Ethan's sword plunged into his stomach. Leaning forward on the blade, Ethan met his gaze. "Watch me."

He yanked the sword out and Kieran cupped both hands over the wound, blood leaking through his fingers.

The smell of his own blood made everything sway and his stomach tumbled in protest. Kieran took in short breaths and then let out short pants.

Ethan turned away and howled loudly at noticing Gisela was not where she'd been. He rushed to the spot and looked around. Then he went to the edge of the crest and peered down.

"Bitch!" he yelled and raced past the spot to look for her. Kieran scrambled to his feet. The entire time, his body protested. He picked up his sword.

Just then, Ethan bent at the waist and dragged a struggling Gisela from behind a boulder. Kieran came from behind, but Ethan caught sight of him and lifted the sword, pointing it toward him.

They were too close to the ridge's edge and Kieran didn't dare attack. It would be too easy for Ethan to push Gisela over the edge.

She attempted to push Ethan's hand away from where he held her hair. Gisela's gaze lifted to him and, in her eyes, he saw determination. The woman was going to fight for her life. Silently, she mouthed, "Help me."

"Guards come this way and will arrive soon," Kieran said, taking a step closer. "Even if ye kill us both, ye cannot get away. There is only one path down and my men will catch ye."

Ethan stopped in his tracks and narrowed his eyes. "No one comes. Ye always travel alone."

As if making a point, a flock of birds burst from down the path, noisily flying past them. Ethan craned his neck and looked down.

Kieran took two steps closer. "Let her go. Ye want me, not her."

"Ye are already dying," Ethan stated. "She must die. I want ye to see it."

Gisela focused on where Kieran's bloody hand pressed to his stomach.

"Stop this madness," Gisela cried out. "Ye cannot think to get away with all of this."

"I can and I will," Ethan spouted, loosening his hold on her hair to thrust the sword in Kieran's direction. "That is close enough."

Gisela punched Ethan between the legs so hard that he cried out, dropped his sword and fell to his knees.

"Bastard!" she yelled.

Kieran hurried forward and kicked the sword away from Ethan.

"I still win!" Ethan slowly stood and held both arms out.

It took several seconds before Kieran realized what the madman meant to do. Kieran closed the distance between them, grabbing at Ethan's tunic. But he was too late. Ethan fell backward off the ridge and plunged to his death.

"No," Kieran gritted the word out. He hadn't been the one to kill Ethan; the bastard had not given him the opportunity.

Unsure what to do, he dropped to his knees. If death decided to claim him, he was more than ready.

Kieran lay next to a fire Gisela had started hours earlier. They didn't speak much. Although she was weak, she'd bound his wounds with strips from her underskirts and, thankfully, blood no longer seeped through. They'd managed to get back to his mount. Unfortunately, Kieran being too weak from injuries combined with Gisela's lack of nourishment, neither had the energy to mount Laith.

After drinking from a wineskin and eating dried meats Kieran had packed, they huddled by the fire. hoping the smoke and flames would alert the guards of where they were.

Gisela was slumped next to where Kieran lay on the ground. She'd inched closer to him, touched his shoulder. "How do ye feel?"

Dragging his eyes up to her, he wasn't sure how to respond. What could he say? That he felt empty, unsatisfied? The fall had killed his enemy instantly. No suffering, no last moments clutching to life. It had been quick, all of it.

Ethan McLeod's death should fill him with satisfaction. Instead, it was as if all the sense of living had been sucked from his body, leaving behind an empty shell. No feelings, sensations or care penetrated that shell. Whether he lived or died in that moment meant nothing to him.

There it was, what he'd been warned about. Seeking revenge and finally getting it did not bring his father back, nor did it seem enough to repay what had happened.

It was only when looking into Gisela's eyes that something buried deep inside him flickered. But like a candle against a gust of wind, he could not keep it from burning out.

"Try yer best not to pass out, please," Gisela pleaded and her eyes filled with tears. "Ye have to remain alive."

He'd never seen her so vulnerable, so gaunt. Although still beautiful, she was in need of care. She required a hot bath, good food and a soft bed.

"Ye? How do ye feel?" He spoke in a quiet, flat tone as it was impossible to generate any kind of emotion.

She nodded, a frown marring her brow. "I am fine."

It was obvious she wasn't by the faraway flatness of her tone. But he didn't have the energy to ask more. Soon, he lost the ability to keep from it and allowed blackness to envelope him.

CHAPTER TWENTY

IT WAS LATE, the sun already setting by the time the guards arrived. Thankfully, they'd thought ahead and brought a wagon. She wondered if they'd planned to take one or two bodies back to the keep.

Gisela kept her eyes closed, not wishing to have a conversation with anyone. The last days were not something she wanted to dwell upon, much less speak to anyone about.

Although Kieran had awakened several times, he did not speak to her. Instead, he'd kept his gaze fixed on the passing scenery. He had to be in horrible pain; the injuries were many, most of them deep cuts, especially the one to his stomach.

A healer had come with the guards. He'd tended to Kieran after she'd insisted she was well.

She studied Kieran now. Every time the wagon drove over a bumpy patch, his brow scrunched. At the moment, he slept, his handsome face smeared with dirt and blood.

Reaching over, she swept hair off his brow and then settled back against the side of the wagon, depleted.

Soon, summer would arrive. Normally, it was her favorite time of year, when she would sit in the village square, sell soap and chat with villagers who passed by. The days passed quickly and she'd enjoyed the interactions between the village people and highborn people who traveled there to do their weekly shopping.

Once a week, she and her mother would go to visit with Lady Munro and have a meal in the great room with other clanspeople, her mother ensuring that everyone knew they were related.

Interesting that at the moment, the little things that had annoyed her, she now longed for. Sure she'd be dead, she had prayed fervently for God to spare her and that she'd do her best to make others happy. That she would love her mother and brother and tend to the sick and poor.

And she had survived. Even though her body was so weak that it took monumental energy to just sit upright, she was alive.

The experience was one she'd not ever forget. The madman's face would forever be etched on her mind. Gisela took deep gulps of air to keep from sobbing.

She'd been slapped, dragged, kicked and starved for the entire time and yet she'd fought to stay alive. Now that it was over, the sensation of wanting to roll up in a ball and allow life to ebb didn't make sense.

"Gisela?" Someone spoke and she realized she'd fallen asleep. Dragging her eyes open, Ceilidh's face came into view.

"Ye're safe now, dear." Ceilidh held her right hand and gave a light tug. The woman had climbed atop the wagon with a large guard who lifted her easily. He then lowered Gisela to another who carried her toward the keep.

"Kieran?" she whispered to the man.

"Inside being looked after by the healer," he replied.

The next time Gisela woke, she was in a comfortable bed inside a small but nice bedchamber. Ceilidh and Merida sat in chairs next to a narrow window, speaking in soft tones. She studied the women for a moment and considered how she would have liked to remain there and become part of the closely-knit group.

However, once she was strong enough, Kieran would ensure she returned home. It was for the best, he had a great deal of healing to do, not just physically, but internally as well.

LATER THAT DAY, the women helped her bathe and then ensured she ate a sturdy meal of porridge with bits of meat. Having eaten, soaked in hot water and had her hair untangled, Gisela felt human again.

"I need to see Kieran. He saved my life."

The women exchanged an undecipherable look.

Her stomach sank. "Oh, no…is he…"

"He is alive and will recover," Merida said in a flat tone. Gisela was aware the woman and Kieran did not speak, so she understood the lack of care.

Ceilidh studied her for a long moment. "Perhaps it will be good for ye to see him. He has not spoken a word since returning. I am afraid of his reaction at seeing ye. He has always been such a mystery to us."

"Let's wait until ye have had a bit more time to recover yerself," Merida finally said.

The next day, Gisela rose and went to the mirror. She looked absolutely horrible. There was a frightening combination of purple and yellow bruising on the left side of her face. The left temple was swollen where she'd fallen onto the ground, or perhaps when her captor had hit her with the hilt of his sword. Her bottom lip was split, dried blood encrusted across it.

Her hair had been brushed back and braided, which was good as her right arm ached from being kicked. Her ribs smarted when Gisela took sharp breaths, although the binding helped.

After managing to don a robe, she walked out of the room and headed to Kieran's chamber, which was just a bit down the narrow corridor.

She pushed the door open slowly and peered into the room. The chamber was dark with long, thick curtains drawn over the windows. The air was stale and smelled of smoke from the fire in the hearth.

There was no one watching over Kieran at the moment,

which was understandable as he pushed people away.

Kieran lay on his back, eyes closed, a slight frown marring his face. There were beads of sweat on his upper lip and forehead. Someone should have opened the window and left the door open to allow for air to flow.

"This is ridiculous," Gisela mumbled. She went to the window and, using only her left hand, pulled the curtains open. The sun brightened the room immediately. She pushed the window open, which took effort as she could only use one arm, but determination won and, instantly, she was greeted with a soft breeze.

Kieran did not stir.

Allowing her gaze to travel down his face to the top of his bare chest, she noted cuts, bruises and bandaging.

"Kieran," she whispered. "Wake up."

His eyes fluttered open and the hazel gaze slid to her face. He didn't speak as his eyes traveled down across her face, hesitating at the injuries.

Gisela sat on the edge of his bed and let out a long sigh. "Ye saved my life." Her voice broke and she hesitated. "Thank ye."

Kieran swallowed visibly and closed his eyes. Did he wish her gone? Or was he merely too weak? Gisela touched his arm.

"Once I recover, I will take ye home." Kieran's voice was flat.

The words were like daggers, hurting more than the injuries. Gisela let out a breath. It came out sharp like when someone was punched in the stomach.

"I see. Ye do not have to. I can ask to be taken home right away. There is no need to wait."

What had she expected from Kieran, a request for her to marry him or some sort of declaration that he loved her?

Gisela studied him. He looked...defeated.

"Ye have finally gotten yer revenge. Avenged yer father's death. I am glad for ye."

He flinched as if she'd struck him with a hot iron straight from a fire.

Not sure what else to do, she stood and limped back to the door. Just as she reached it, Gisela looked back to the bed one last time. Kieran's eyes were fixed on her and then he closed them again.

CHAPTER TWENTY-ONE

Late summer

"I CERTAINLY DO not understand why ye came back," her mother exclaimed as Gisela mixed the ingredients for a new batch of soap. "Ye are betrothed to Kieran Ross and he must keep his word and marry ye."

They were outside in a small courtyard at her mother's home in the village. Gisela had gone straight there upon returning. The first days had been wonderfully quiet as her mother had been at the keep.

It was exactly what she'd needed to settle her mind and return to life without Kieran.

"He never asked to marry me, Mother," Gisela repeated for what seemed like the hundredth time. "The first thing he said at seeing me after the rescue, was that he'd bring me home once he recovered."

Her mother huffed. "Nevertheless, ye should have remained."

"I was not going to remain at Ross Keep. There was no reason for it."

"If he was not going to keep his word, he should have sent ye back with enough coin to survive and not have to sell yer wares at the village square like some sort of pauper." Her mother sniffed and wiped at an imaginary tear.

"He never asked me to marry me, Mother."

Her mother made a slashing motion with her right hand. "It was implied upon the invitation to go to his keep."

Kieran hadn't even been aware she traveled to Dun Airgid. However, there was no use in telling her mother. There was no reasoning with her when she became upset.

"My poor daughter. Who will marry ye now?" Lillian fell back into the chair. "What will come of ye?"

"I assure ye, I will find a man to marry soon. Do not fret. I have several in mind already."

Brightening, Lillian lifted her cup of cider and sipped. "How grand. I will inform Lady Munro immediately upon yer decision so the laird forces the man in question to marry ye without haste."

Gisela wanted to roll her eyes, but forced a smile instead. "What about ye? What happened with the traveling merchant?"

"Oh, he was only a distraction from the obvious," her mother stated and hesitated to give Gisela time to ask.

"What is the obvious, Mother?"

"That I should marry a visiting laird or such or perhaps a guard and live at the keep. I am family after all."

Gisela pictured the guardsmen and could not think of any that were her mother's age, and also unmarried. "Of course, Mother."

The conversations with her mother distracted Gisela from thinking too much about Kieran. She worried about his reaction to Ethan McLeod's death. Why had he been left so hollow? It was as if his reason for living were snatched away the instant the madman had fallen to his death.

Perhaps it was. What would happen to him now?

"Tomorrow, we shall go to the market and spend time with our friends. I am quite excited." Her mother's change in countenance never ceased to amaze her. The woman leaned forward, pinning her with an eager look.

"I have some news," her mother said with an exaggerated heavy sigh. "Ye no longer can aspire to marry Caylen Munro."

Gisela fought not to grin. "Oh? Why is that, Mother?"

"He is betrothed. I suppose the poor boy found another to get over his broken heart. Ye hurt him deeply, I do believe."

Sometimes, Gisela wondered how her mother could weave such a different world for herself that was so very different than reality. It was a nice world, she conceded, albeit a bit strange.

"And who is the lucky woman?"

"A Mackenzie. Laird Munro is thrilled over the alliance with the clan. Although it is to one of the smaller Mackenzie clans, it is still quite an accomplishment. Lady Munro is planning several celebrations leading up to the wedding."

"I am happy for all of them."

"Yes, indeed." Her mother than took her hands. "Oh, and I have even better news."

Her stomach clenched. Whenever her mother came up with something, it was rarely good. "I cannot wait to hear."

"We have been given a set of chambers in the keep. Lady Munro insists we be on hand to assist with all that has to be done."

"Mother," Gisela tried, but failed to keep her voice down. "We have perfect living quarters here in the village. Yer house as well as my cottage are both empty. Besides, the keep is over-crowded and smelly."

Her mother smiled indulgently. "It will be easier for us to find husbands there."

Lillian patted Gisela's cheek. "Besides, Caylen and his portion of the staff will be moving to another smaller home. He is second born after all and cannot expect to remain there."

"But interloping relatives can?" Gisela mumbled. Her mother ignored her, already scanning the space for what she intended to take with her.

CHAPTER TWENTY-TWO

THE CLANGING OF metal against metal as the guards practiced rang in the air. Kieran stood just a short distance away, watching. He and a team of archers had just finished their own target practice and his right arm felt heavy. It had been a long time since he'd practiced, since he'd done much of anything actually.

Amazingly, the recovery from his injuries had been swift, but his desire to do more than eat and amble about the keep had lasted longer.

Keeping to himself and not a man who'd ever been approachable, most left him be. Of course, his brothers had not been as inclined.

Even now, Tristan walked toward him. Kieran braced for the same questions. *What would ye like to do? Is there something ye wish to talk about?*

Tristan grinned widely, throwing Kieran off balance. His brother usually approached tentatively, as if trying to decide how to form his words.

"Ye will never guess who I just saw in the village and brought here." Tristan chuckled and shook his head. "Go on guess."

"How in the hell would I know?"

"Ewan."

Kieran stared at Tristan for a moment. "Ewan Ross, our cousin?"

"Aye," Tristan replied with another chuckle. "He is here now, visiting with Malcolm."

Turning to the main keep, Kieran narrowed his eyes. "Why is he here?"

"He is asking to remain here for a period of time, something about needing to get away."

Despite his sour mood, Kieran was looking forward to see his cousin. They'd practically grown up together. Ewan's family had moved off the western shores of Scotland to the Hebrides almost twenty years earlier and they'd not seen each other much since.

Tristan leaned against the wall and huffed, his expression changing. "Now that Ewan will be here, ye and he will become close again. That will leave me without a sparring partner."

"Ye always spar against Ruari," Kieran replied. "We always end up brawling and Da…" He stopped at realizing their father was no longer there to break them apart.

"True," Tristan said, obviously looking to distract him. Then he suggested, "Want to spar with me now?"

Kieran considered it. He was not recovered enough for it, but he would not admit it to Tristan. His brother was huge. Although Kieran had the advantage of height, Tristan was muscular and broad.

"Very well."

"Ha!" Tristan exclaimed, pulling his sword.

Moving a bit slower, Kieran drew his sword. The first clang of swords sent vibrations down his arm and into his chest. Kieran's lips curved. His brother was not being gentle in the least.

Within minutes, he was drenched in sweat, his sword arm on fire. Exhausted from the short sparring session, Kieran stumbled backward and swore.

Tristan lowered his sword. "Let us go see our cousin."

"Let's." Kieran felt good.

THE MOON WAS full, making it easy to see. Kieran had skipped last meal and taken his meal in the kitchens. Now, he ambled just outside to the vegetable garden.

"Ye have to join with the family and take part in things," Moira said, walking up to him. "'Tis long enough that ye mourn yer father, dear boy."

The woman always treated him like a child. But for some reason, it didn't bother him. He loved Moira, her soft yet firm voice and the way she smelled of herbs and spices.

"I am empty." The statement surprised him. But he continued, unable to stop from it. "I thought the bastard's death would help but, instead, I am angrier. He did not suffer enough."

Moira stood beside him and looked up at the sky. "Ye could have drawn and quartered him and still it would not have been enough. No matter how much he would have suffered, it could never make up for the pain ye felt at seeing yer da be slain."

"I want him back." A tear slipped down his cheek, and Kieran ignored it. "My da was not supposed to die that day."

"He was, darling," Moira said. "We each have a destiny that includes the day we are to die. I believe it to be so. Whether by another's hand or other means, fate claims us at the appointed time."

"Then why does it feel so wrong? He was scared, was not ready…" He'd never told anyone about that day. About the terror in his father's eyes, his pleas for help.

Moira remained quiet. The woman was wise and had known he needed to think things through.

The last words his father had spoken had been pleas for his help. And although he'd tried to help, it had been fruitless.

He'd failed his father by not saving him, by not protecting him. It didn't matter that he'd sought and gotten revenge. Nothing would ever reverse the fact that he'd not been able to do enough the day Ethan McLeod had struck his father down.

"What should I do?" Kieran finally asked.

"Live abundantly. Take yer revenge by not giving Ethan more power over yer life than ye already have. It is what yer da would have wanted."

A star fell across the dark sky and he followed its descent. It was that star's destiny to go out that night.

"I will try," he said, turning to find that Moira had left.

"I EXPECTED YE would be married as well," Ewan said as he and Kieran made their way through a dense thicket in search of the deer they hunted. "Everyone seems to be."

Kieran shrugged. "Ye're not."

His cousin's laughter reminded him of the carefree time when, as youths, they'd often hunted in the same forest. "I am not the kind of man to settle."

There were many men who preferred not to be with one woman. Ewan claimed to be one who enjoyed different women, not being tied down.

There was a sound ahead. They stopped in their tracks and listened intently. A buck sprung from behind a tree and both of them pulled back on their bows and shot.

"Now to track him." Kieran hurried after the buck, his cousin on his heels. It occurred to him that it had been a long time since he'd enjoyed himself.

His boots crunched on fallen leaves, the whispers of branches whizzed past his ears as he ran. Birds fluttered away, their chirps announcing displeasure at being rousted.

A family of rabbits scampered away, then stopped and watched at noting they were not being chased.

Kieran pushed back low branches and continued following the buck's trail. With heavy footfalls, his cousin's location was easy to track. Right behind him, Ewan seemed to find every single branch to run into.

By the time they found the fallen buck, both were breathless. The grin on Ewan's face almost made Kieran smile.

"I felled him," Ewan announced, pulling what remained of an arrow from the buck's neck.

Kieran inspected it. "That is one of mine."

Ewan inspected the arrow and shrugged, throwing it over his shoulder. "It could be, but we will not know for sure."

It had always been like that between them. Although they competed, they rarely sought glee in besting each other.

Working together, they made a cot of sorts to drag the animal back, the entire time reminiscing of times past.

"I am glad I came," Ewan said. "I do hate that Uncle Robert is no longer here, but tis nice all the same."

At the mention of his father, Kieran waited for the familiar pang of guilt to strike. It was slow and made his chest clench, but it wasn't as strong as he expected.

"I am glad that ye came as well," Kieran said, meaning it.

"We should go to the village to celebrate," Ewan said later as they almost reached the edge of the forest. "Any pretty lasses ye can introduce me to?"

Considering most people gave him wide berth, Kieran almost laughed. "I am not the one to ask. Ruari, he would go with ye."

Ewan studied him. "Ye do enjoy the company of women, do ye not?"

Resisting the urge to growl at the insinuation, Kieran nodded. "Aye, of course."

"Ah," Ewan said, shaking his head.

Whatever his cousin was thinking, Kieran shouldn't care, but he couldn't help but ask. "What does that mean?"

"There is one lass in particular ye save yerself for."

"Save myself. Ye sound as if I am a virginal sot." Kieran wanted to punch Ewan in the face. Instead, he huffed and continued walking forward. A picture of a wide-eyed and wild-haired Gisela clinging to him formed. He did miss her.

"Tell me about her," Ewan prodded.

Kieran thought for a moment. There was no harm, he supposed, in describing Gisela to his cousin. It wasn't as if he'd ever see her again.

"She is like this buck. Strong and untamable. Her eyes are dark, while at the same time lightening when she is happy. When she talks, she uses her entire body to make a point. Although she doesn't try, she is graceful, kind and alluring." Kieran stopped talking, noticing Ewan watched him intently with a questioning expression.

"Ye're in love." His cousin threw his head back and laughed.

"I am not. I admire her. That is all."

Ewan shook his head. "I wish to meet this alluring creature immediately."

"She lives in the north, a Munro."

"We shall go then," Ewan announced.

Kieran started to say no, then surprised himself. "Aye, we should go."

CHAPTER TWENTY-THREE

G ISELA'S MOTHER HAD accepted an invitation to the tavern in the village and dragged her along. Protests had not worked and, finally, Gisela decided that perhaps if her mother found a husband, the woman would leave her be.

At the moment, Gisela was leaning back, wishing there was a way to get further from the man who sat next to her. Besides constantly staring at her chest, he breathed heavily through his mouth, which was a pity since his breath reeked.

Her mother, on the other hand, was delighted at the attention he and his father now gave them. "Tell me, Hamish," she gushed at the father. "How is it we have never met ye and yer handsome son?"

Gisela studied the younger man. Handsome was not a way to describe him. He had a short nub for a nose, round cheeks and lips that drooped down at the corners. How in the world had her mother thought she would ever find anything about the man attractive?

"Jonah and I have been traveling extensively," the elderly man stated. He smiled down at her mother's cleavage. "I would never have put off this meeting if I'd known such beauty existed in my own village."

When Jonah placed a hand on Gisela's knee, she pinched it. Hard. He frowned and leaned closer to her ear. "I can hire a room upstairs."

Gisela considered if slapping the idiot would ruin her mother's chances at finding a new husband.

When Jonah's leg pressed against her thigh, she elbowed him in the ribs with force.

The man grimaced, but his lips curved and he leaned close to her ear. "I do prefer my women fiery."

Had the man actually bedded women who weren't paid to be with him? She felt sorry for them. Both the paid and unpaid.

"Get away from me," she hissed under her breath. "I am not interested."

"Both ye and yer mother seek husbands. Why not us?" His gaze moved over her as if assessing what she looked like without clothing.

Gisela stood abruptly. "I need to see about…something." It wasn't far but she hoped to make it out the front door.

Unfortunately, Jonah stood as well. Did the idiot think she was actually interested enough to go upstairs with him. She glared at him. "Alone."

"Nonsense, I will accompany ye."

Her mother smiled widely up at her. "Enjoy yer walk, darling."

Gisela stalked toward the front of the small tavern but stopped when a large man blocked her exit. He stood with his arms crossed and a wide grin on his face. "Ye seem to be in need of rescue."

Unfortunately, the abrupt stop meant Jonah came up behind and bumped against Gisela. He did not move backward. Instead, he breathed at the back of her neck.

Perhaps in the future, being squashed between two men would be comical. At the moment, it was not.

Gisela had to tilt her head back to see her would-be rescuer's face. "No, I do not require rescue. What I require is for ye to get out of my way."

There was a hint of surprise at her lack of being overcome by his size and handsome face. She'd had enough handsome, or grotesque for that matter, to last her a lifetime.

"Kindly step aside," Gisela said. Then jabbing her elbow backward, she spoke over her shoulder, "If ye do not get away from me, I will kick ye to death."

This time, the stranger began to laugh. He stepped aside. "Ye are right, Cousin. She is breathtaking."

Kieran entered and stood just inside the doorway. His face was expressionless as always, but there was a calm about him. His brow was as smooth as a loch in the winter.

Everyone in the tavern watched him, fascinated by the beauty of the man. There were murmurs as everyone took notice of Kieran and the man who'd called him cousin. The room became deadly silent.

"Ye're back," Gisela said and let out a breath. She stepped up to him and looked from his face down his chest to his feet. "Looks like ye healed well. I'm glad to see it."

She rounded him and walked outside. Gulping air, she couldn't stop the hammering of her heart. Why had he come? It was impossible to move on since he'd decided to appear out of nowhere.

"Gisela?"

His deep voice pierced her skin, making her entire body vibrate. Gisela didn't respond. Instead, she reached for the wall of the tavern. It wouldn't do for her knees to give out and make a fool out of herself by swooning.

"Why are ye here?" She grimaced at the trembling of her voice. Hopefully, he would mistake it for annoyance.

She did not want to appear weak and definitely not overcome by the fact she'd been harboring a deep desire to see him again. She'd not admitted it to even herself, but now it was impossible to deny it. She'd missed him terribly.

"My cousin, Ewan, who ye just met and I are headed to Munro Keep." He studied her for a long moment. "How are ye?"

Ignoring the question, she looked past him to where the large blond man stood. "Why come through the village?"

Before speaking, he took a step forward. "We wanted to stop and drink at the tavern before going to the keep."

For some reason, it didn't sound convincing. Gisela shrugged. "Very well then. Enjoy."

"Where are ye going?"

She looked to the sky. Fluffy white clouds floated in the bright blue expanse. A gentle breeze blew, giving just a hint that perhaps it would be a chilly night. It was interesting that outwardly the world continued normally, while hers was spinning.

"Home."

He started to say something and then cleared his throat. "I hoped to see ye."

She met his gaze, the thickly lashed hazel gaze that she'd dreamed of nightly since last seeing him.

The ever-present scowl appeared at her perusal. He was so utterly beautiful and now he seemed lighter, more approachable. To anyone but her. Gisela felt the urge to cry.

Physically perfect and yet so inwardly imperfect was who Kieran was. She doubted he would ever change. He was the man she could envision spending the rest of her life with, the one who'd shelter her, providing a safe haven just with his presence alone. He'd shattered her heart and at the same time made it full.

"Why?"

He blinked as if taken aback by her question. "To see about ye. How ye fared..." Kieran looked over his shoulder to the now empty doorway. Obviously, his cousin had become bored and had gone inside.

"Would ye come to the keep with me?"

Munro Keep had been her home for the last few weeks. She'd been staying there and spending time helping with one event after another. Lady Munro never seemed to tire of hosting and, unfortunately, had decided she and her mother were indispensable. As annoying as it was, the constant activity had been the perfect distraction.

"I live there now."

He nodded. "I see. Is that man at the doorway yer…"

"No," she replied much too quickly, noticing Jonah glaring at them from just outside the doorway.

"Wait here," Kieran said, holding a hand out as if afraid she'd leave. "I will inform yer mother as well that ye go with us."

"There is no need…" she called, but he ignored her.

Gisela let out a breath and waited as Kieran went into the tavern to fetch Ewan. Moments later, the two formidable warriors made their way toward her. Ewan resembled his cousins in size and had the same hazel eyes. His hair was blond.

Upon approaching, Kieran motioned to her with his right hand. "Cousin, this is Gisela Munro. Gisela, my cousin, Ewan Ross."

Ewan's right eyebrow arched, and a hint of a smile played on his lips. With a slight bow, he met her gaze. "Ye're a lovely lass. I can see why my cousin is so fond of ye."

"Fond?" Gisela looked to Kieran who pretended not to hear. "Thank ye, Ewan."

Gisela was flanked by the two men. Everyone stopped and gaped as they passed by. No doubt, people thought she was being escorted off to a dungeon or something. Gisela waved at a group of women who stared. The women did not return the gesture. Instead, they began an animated conversation, motioning in their direction.

"I can hardly wait to hear what people will make of this," Gisela murmured. "I do not require an escort. I have my own horse and cart."

Before she could step away, Kieran took her arm. "I will go with ye." It was best to go along than to fight him at the moment. Not only was his cousin there, but the women continued to watch them, whatever was in their baskets forgotten.

Moments later, seated side-by-side on her wagon, they rode toward the keep. Kieran's horse was tethered to his cousin's, who rode just ahead of them.

"Why are ye living at the keep?" Kieran asked, his gaze forward.

Gisela let out a sigh. "Lady Munro and Mother have come to an agreement that I am indispensable and must assist in the planning of every occasion."

"Is it enjoyable?"

"What?" She looked at him.

"The planning of every occasion."

"I have yet to plan one. Yer mother, my mother and Lady Munro take over." She couldn't help but smile. "I have, however, gotten to know yer sister quite well."

This time, he did turn and study her. "How do ye and Verity get along?"

"Well. She is quiet, but kind."

"I am glad to hear that my mother and sister are doing well."

Gisela wasn't sure what to make of Kieran's insistence to ride with her to Munro Keep. He seemed different and then again not so much. Although the same feeling of comfort filled her with him there, at the same time, she'd not gotten through the high, thick walls erected around him.

"How are yer injuries? Ye look well healed," she prompted.

Eyes remaining on the road, his right shoulder lifted and lowered. "I am well."

"What now? Have ye considered what ye'll do now?" she prodded.

There was a spark of interest in his gaze when he slid a glance at her, brow lowered.

As he seemed to be waiting for whatever she'd planned to say next, Gisela continued. "He's dead. Ye must feel vindicated. However, life goes on, as they say. So ye should have a new quest in mind," she finished, willing her tone to remain even, cheerful almost.

"I," he looked to his cousin as if to ensure he was out of earshot. "I have many duties to the clan."

"I see. What else?" Gisela replied. "Yer father, I am sure, would be proud…"

This time, he pulled the reins tight and her horse came to an abrupt stop and protested the jerk at its bridle. When Ewan turned back, Kieran motioned for him to continue forth.

"I do not wish to discuss my father," Kieran scowled at her.

"And I do not tolerate any mistreatment of animals." She jumped from the wagon and hurried to soothe her horse who gave her a hurt look. The animal was pampered and rarely chastised even when acting inappropriately.

"There, there." Gisela ran a hand over the animal's nose and kissed the mare. Kieran waited in the cart, stubbornly looking straight ahead.

She took her time walking back to the cart. Then she climbed up to sit beside the brooding man. "If ye promise to treat Rosebud well, I will allow ye to continue to guide her. Otherwise, hand me the reins."

"I apologize," he replied and then continued speaking, to her surprise. "I have not spoken of what happened other than to inform everyone he is dead."

"Ethan McLeod was a madman. He had no true reason for his hatred of yer family other than a misguided cause to kill everyone based on jealousy. He could not stop speaking of how much he hated ye and how ye and yer brothers thought yerselves above others."

Kieran remained quiet, his jaw clenched. "Did he speak of my father?" he finally gritted out.

"No. It was as if he'd forgotten about it." Gisela placed a hand on his forearm. "He planned to kill his own family as well. He said he hated his father for preferring Alec over him."

"He was truly mad then." Kieran finally looked at her. For the first time, there was vulnerability. So many questions. She had no idea what he was thinking. However, she understood that his entire reason for being since his father's death was gone now.

"Ye have done well," she said. "Yer father would be proud of how ye vowed to avenge his death and fulfilled the promise. I know I am very thankful to ye for saving my life." Her eyes welled and she leaned forward and kissed his jaw.

Kieran grunted. "Tis good to know ye soothe me the same as yer horse."

Gisela couldn't help it. She giggled and then turned his face. Once again, she kissed him. This time, on the lips. It was a quick kiss, like that of friends or lovers familiar with each other enough to share soft, sweet kisses.

"I do not kiss Rosebud on the lips. That, I promise ye."

A smile played at his lips. Gisela watched, hoping for a full smile. Finally, when the corners of his mouth inched up, she grinned back.

Satisfied to see he was no longer brooding, she once again placed a hand on his forearm. "I have something to show ye tonight when the stars come out. I think ye will like it."

He snapped the reins gently and they continued on their way. "I hope there are no celebrations planned this week. I am hoping for some quiet."

"Then ye came to the wrong place. Yer mother and Lady Munro are hosting the Mackenzies who came with about twenty."

He groaned and Gisela laughed. "I am sure ye will find plenty of places to hide."

Kieran gave her a side look. "Can I hide with ye?"

Her cheeks burned hot and she looked away toward an open field. "Perhaps ye can go for walks or practice with the archers. I am sure that upon yer arrival, my uncle and the Mackenzie will insist there be a competition."

"So ye won't allow me to hide with ye then?" he insisted.

Was he flirting with her? Gisela's eyebrows rose. "If I do, will ye promise to behave like a gentleman?"

"I am not sure I can," he replied. He leaned over and kissed her just below the ear. A shiver went through her and she swallowed. "I see."

He straightened as they'd arrived at the gates. The familiar scowl returned. Although some of the wall had been chipped away, it remained strong and stubborn. It would take years to scale the fortress that surrounded the man, but Gisela considered that she may have found a doorway.

Not one she'd carved out, but one he had opened. Just for her.

CHAPTER TWENTY-FOUR

Clan McLeod

ALEC MCLEOD STORMED from the keep. When angry, it was best to walk away rather than to remain in a room and argue. Especially now that it was his own father he was furious at.

It had to be hard for a parent to lose a child, but his father was acting as if Ethan had been a great son. Ethan had never done one thing to make the family proud. Instead, he had been the cause of hundreds of clanspeople perishing. His killing of the Ross Clan's laird had brought rifts that would take years to bridge.

To this day, small clashes and deaths occurred weekly between the clans. Everyone knew that just because a truce was called, it didn't mean sentiments or ill will were magically erased.

He exited the courtyard through a side gate and walked to the edge of the woods. It was then he noticed one of his hounds, a newly acquired pup, had followed at his heels. The animal was delighted at the new surroundings and began to explore, his nose to the ground and tail wagging.

He wished he could be like the pup with the only cares being when to be fed and where to sleep.

Keeping an eye on the dog to ensure it didn't wander too far,

Alec continued walking until he came to a shallow creek. He lowered to sit on a fallen tree.

Just then, his wife, a beautiful vision, came into view. She walked toward him from the water.

Later, he would admonish her for going out alone. It was dangerous for the wife of the laird's first-born son to be out and about without escort. But for now, he admired her and watched as the pup rushed to her, yapping and wagging not only his tail, but also his entire body.

She smiled and ran her fingers through the dog's fur before realizing that the pup must be with someone. Paige looked up and met his gaze. Her lips curved and she opened her arms to him.

Alec neared and wrapped his arms around her. He lifted his wife off her feet so he could bury his face in her hair.

"We cannot help how people grieve, dear one," Paige said, holding him tightly. "Especially when it is one's child. A father would rather his son be remembered as a good man."

She must have heard the argument between him and his father and had come out here to get away from it.

When his tears fell, Alec realized he had not grieved his brother's death. Too much anger coursed through him at everything Ethan had done. All the wrongs and horrible words he'd spewed at him and the family. But Ethan was ill, his mind unwell. It wasn't something that could have been helped.

Alec grieved.

Not for who Ethan had become, but for the younger brother who'd tagged behind him as a child, constantly chattering, looking up to him as if he were a champion. For a few years, he had been. His little brother's champion. He'd stopped trying a long time ago. Hopefully, in the end, Ethan had a bit of clarity and hadn't hated his own family any longer.

Dun Airgid: Ross Keep

CEILIDH WOKE TO find Ian next to her in bed. Sometime during the night, he had come to her bed, slid under the bedding and fallen into an exhausted slumber.

It was improper for them to sleep together, but they'd given up the pretense and no longer hid it from the household.

Elspeth had tried to talk her out of it, claiming her family would be angry. But they rarely came to the keep and when they did, it was during the day, which would give Ian and her time to make other arrangements.

Stretching, she turned to Ian and studied his face. In just a week, they would be married. Husband and wife. Every morning for the rest of their lives, she would wake next to the man she loved lying beside her.

His eyes opened, the clear blue-green gaze just a bit hazy from not being fully awake. Then his lips curved and her heart melted.

"Go back to sleep," she said, kissing him. "Tis quite early yet. The sun has not fully risen."

She snuggled against him, inhaling the smell of him. He was so large and muscled and yet felt comforting and sure. He lay on his left side, the one with the missing arm. Part of it anyway. It had been severed just above the elbow. He had begun using it with a specially made shield that Elspeth's father, who was a blacksmith, had fashioned for him. Ian was proud of how he was able to pull it from the side of the horse and hoist it up and across to shield from attack.

For days, he'd been using it at sword practice, which explained his exhaustion.

"What are ye thinking about?" His voice had the husky tone from just waking.

"That ye come to bed exhausted every night since ye got the shield. Elspeth's father has come up with the perfect way to keep us from making love."

Ian chuckled. "Has he?" He rolled to his back, bringing her across his body. "Have ye considered how to make love to me?"

At first, she wasn't sure what he meant, then it became clear. If he could take her while she lay on her back, then she could take him as well.

First, she pushed back the bedding then lifted up and straddled him. She ran her hands down his chest, enjoying how his skin felt and the slight tightening of each place she touched.

His reactions emboldened her to do more, so she trailed kisses down the center of his body while reaching for his sex. He was hard and ready.

Ceilidh looked to see that he was watching intently.

It took a bit of maneuvering, but she managed to lift and guide him in. He seemed perfectly comfortable allowing her freedom over his body and did not assist her in the least.

It was an enjoyable game, Ceilidh decided, and she lowered, taking him fully.

At joining, both of them let out loud moans.

Moments later, she panted, and her body sprawled over his. Ian kissed her temple. "I love ye with my entire being."

The words seeped into her, renewing her. Love, she decided, was the balm to sooth and the energy that willed a person to grow.

CHAPTER TWENTY-FIVE

AFTER GREETING KIERAN fondly, his mother and sister quickly became engrossed with Ewan. He'd always held a spell over them, with his elaborate gifts, quick wit and spilling of compliments.

They sat in the large sitting room, accompanied by Verity's companion and Lady Munro. Of course, Ewan had also brought Lady Munro a beautifully embroidered handkerchief and the woman pronounced it to be a new prized possession.

Kieran sat near a window overlooking a side garden that flourished with many vegetables and herbs. He wondered if Gisela worked there.

"When do ye plan to marry the poor girl?" His mother stood next to the window, pinning him with a stern look.

Of course, she meant Gisela, or at least that's what he assumed.

Before he could reply, she continued. "She is yer betrothed after all and no other young man will approach her. The poor thing will be left a spinster, spending her days mending castaways."

It was hard to picture Gisela sitting in a corner mending.

"Why do ye think she and I are betrothed?"

"It was deemed so by the laird and she went to Dun Airgid with Tristan and his party. Presumably that means ye and she have…"

"We have not and she is not." Kieran got to his feet, not quite sure why the thought of betrothal bothered him so much.

The room became quiet, every eye on him now.

"The girl is ruined nonetheless," his mother said with a sad shake of her head.

"If ye do not wish to marry my niece, I will ensure her uncle sees her married off and gone from here as soon as possible," Lady Munro said and stood. "She is quite lovely and I am sure many will vie for her hand."

"I'll marry her," Ewan said with a wide grin. "She is indeed lovely."

Kieran couldn't believe his ears. His cousin was no closer to marriage than any man he'd ever met. Ewan had always professed to remain single and without ties.

"Ye will not," Kieran said. He then looked to Lady Munro who gave him a questioning look.

Lady Munro let out a sigh. "If not yer cousin, then a Mackenzie. There are plenty here visiting." She smiled fondly at Ewan. "I will ensure a chamber is prepared for ye and Kieran. Now, I must be off to find Gisela and then my husband."

Upon the woman's departure, his family didn't speak. Instead, they all watched him with varying looks of disapproval.

"Why would ye say that?" Kieran snapped at Ewan. "Ye are not ready for marriage."

"Says who?" Ewan retorted. "As a matter of fact, I am of half a mind to go after the dear lady and insist that it be me."

Kieran fought the urge to punch his cousin's face in. "Do what ye wish. But ye will not marry Gisela."

He hurried from the room, not exactly sure where he was heading. The entire plan for the day was to remain away from people. It was a matter of protocol to visit for several days before leaving. It would give Ewan time with his mother and sister and him time for solitary archery practice.

At the idea, he decided to retrieve his bow and quiver.

He passed what looked to be a small chamber and noticed the door open. Just inside, he saw her. Gisela stood next to a window, a small sack in one hand as she craned to search out the courtyard below.

"Good, he is nowhere to be seen," she murmured. Then she stretched and searched again.

"Who are ye avoiding?"

Gisela yelped and dropped the small sack. Her eyes rounded and she held both hands to her chest.

Gisela being dressed in a plain frock with frayed hems meant she planned to go traipsing in the forest.

"I am not avoiding anyone." The coloring of her cheeks contradicted her words.

He pushed the door closed with his foot, as it would not do for someone to see him inside a single woman's chambers. She was unescorted after all.

"What are ye doing?" She took a step backward.

"Answer my question."

"If ye must know, I did not wish to be seen by a certain man in this plain frock."

His chest constricted. Was she in love with someone else? Had she forgotten about him? He was assuming she had cared for him, perhaps she hadn't.

She'd closed the distance between them and they stood but mere inches apart. "All for naught since ye have seen me now."

There was the hesitance of a woman unsure of how to proceed with a man when her arms encircled his neck and she pulled him down for a kiss.

It was not their first one. But by the way his entire body tightened, it felt as if he were to be kissed for the first time in his life.

She hesitated again, her eyes meeting his, asking, seeking permission. Or perhaps she needed encouragement.

Closing the distance, he took her mouth and, immediately, heat surged to every part of him. Only Gisela could affect him with but a touch of her lips.

The kiss was sweet while at the same time wanton and full of promise. The plushness of her full breasts against his chest and the curves of her womanly body beneath his palms were like a whirlwind of pure light into his dark world.

He loved Gisela with his entire being. The certainty made him both happy and terrified. What would he do now?

Gisela was the perfect woman for him. But at the same time, could he be what she needed? He had no idea of how to be a husband, a partner or a woman's champion. He'd never been in a relationship since he'd yet to find a woman who'd get past his appearance and truly know him.

Gisela's breathing hitched when Kieran trailed his hands up and down her back. Enjoying the warmth of her supple body against him, he kissed from the corner of her mouth to the place just beneath her jawline.

"I love ye," Gisela said, her words stilted. "Ye don't have to reply with the same, but I thought ye should know," she quickly added.

The tightness in his chest made Kieran push away. Was he about to falter, to drop to his knees?

Eyes wide, Gisela reached out to him. "What is the matter? Ye look like ye are about to pass out."

"I am not going to pass out." His words sounded strangled, like a man gasping his last breath.

"Ye certainly look like it." She tugged his hand and led him to a chair. "Goodness, Kieran, I do not think ye are quite healed yet." She pushed him backward and he fell into a chair.

When a glass of water was pushed into his hand and she urged him to drink, he did. Then he coughed at not quite swallowing properly.

"I will fetch the healer." Gisela studied his face. "Do ye think ye are able to make it out to the corridor? It will not do to admit ye were in here."

Kieran got to his feet, annoyed at looking weak before her. "I am not unwell, just overcome." God, that sounded worse.

"What I mean is that I have to admit something to ye."

Her expression became stricken as if he were about to tell her he loved another and would marry that very same afternoon.

"What is it?" Gisela asked, hitching her chin. "Tell me."

"I love ye. I believe I have for a long time."

Silence stretched as they each tried to decide how to proceed. They loved each other. It was said out loud and now he wondered why it had taken him so long to admit it.

Not only was she a beautiful woman, but she was also the first to get through the well-fortified wall he'd erected around his heart.

Walking closer to him, she leaned against him and he pulled her close. "What do we do now?" she asked, her tone low.

"I have to speak to Lady Munro," he replied, gently pushing her back.

"Lady Munro?" Gisela followed him to the doorway. "Why?"

"I may have led her to believe ye need to be married off."

With strength he didn't know she possessed, Gisela shoved him aside, rushed to the door and hurried out.

He followed after, not quite sure if she was going to stop Lady Munro or just see who she was to be paired to. "Gisela," he called after her, but she waved him away. "Ye have done enough for today, Kieran. Why don't ye go play with arrows or something?"

Play with arrows? He scowled at a guard who chuckled as they walked by.

"We should speak to Lady Munro together," he said as she disappeared around a corner. When he got to the end of the corridor, she was gone.

The woman moved rather quickly when she was angry, he considered. A short distance later, he entered the great room. Gisela, Lady Munro, Gisela's mother and the laird were in a small circle.

Not sure whether to go near, he stood next to the entrance until he spotted Ewan. His cousin gave him a smug look.

"It is a lovely day," a woman said, running her hand down his arm. "Perfect for a walk in the garden."

"I do not wish to walk amongst turnips," he replied, not looking away from Gisela who listened to something her mother said while frowning.

"I meant the flower garden," the woman purred, her hand grasping his. "Come, I will show ye."

He didn't move when she tugged and pulled his hand from hers. He looked to the woman for the first time, noting she was a bit older than him. She was still attractive, but had the air of desperation. She didn't need him, any man would probably do.

"I do not believe I have met ye," he said, glancing toward Ewan who lifted a brow in understanding.

"Eleanor Mackenzie, cousin to the laird," she proclaimed.

As Ewan neared, Kieran motioned to him. "I am Kieran Ross and this is my cousin, Ewan. He has yet to visit the gardens."

The woman assessed Ewan, who gave a curt bow. Her lips curved appreciatively.

As the woman and Ewan walked away, Kieran wondered how many times she'd visited the gardens since arriving.

"Ah, Kieran, we have not had an opportunity to speak. Now it seems we have something to discuss." Laird Munro, Gisela's uncle, had come and stood before him.

The man rocked back on his heels and studied him. "What is this I hear that ye do not want to marry my niece, Gisela," he said, sounding annoyed. "Then I must marry her off promptly. I cannot stand any more harassment from my brother's wife. She is a most annoying creature."

"I will marry her," Kieran replied, scowling in the direction of Gisela's mother. She looked at him with narrowed eyes.

What, exactly, had Gisela told them? "What were they speaking about?" he asked, although normally he wouldn't give a fig.

"Oh, Lillian is encouraging my wife and me to find her daughter a husband. She demanded I convince ye to do it as, according to her, ye have sullied the lass' reputation."

"What of the lass? What is her opinion?"

The laird shrugged as if it were of no consequence. "She said she will marry who she wishes and that we should not involve ourselves in it."

Kieran laughed. "Ah. I will speak to her and we shall marry without delay." At the laird's silence, he rounded the man and walked to Gisela. "I must speak to ye."

She didn't protest as he led her to the laird's study. This time, he left the door open to ensure that there was not any misunderstanding by someone happening by.

Whirling, she glared at him. "Ye do not have to be forced into marrying me. Do not marry me because my family insists on it."

"I want to marry ye," Kieran replied. "I had hoped to propose properly. It seems everyone, including my mother, wish to do it for me."

Letting out a long breath, she smiled. "Ye are going to have to hurry and do something or else I will marry yer cousin. Lady Munro said he is willing."

"Marry me, Gisela." Kieran moved closer.

She took a step backward. "Why?"

"Because I love ye and ye love me," he said, his lips curving. "Is that not reason enough?"

Her head tilted to the right. "Hmm. I suppose it is." A crinkle appeared between her brows. "I like seeing ye smile."

This made him scowl. With a simple smile, the beautiful lass could pierce his armor no matter how fortified.

GISELA COULD NOT describe her wedding as small or intimate. Her mother and Lady Munro had insisted the Mackenzies remain.

Then word was sent out to all the Munro clanspeople. Thankfully, there wasn't time to both send a message to Clan Ross and wait their arrival, so they'd not attend. It didn't seem to matter because Lady Ross had made it clear she was not eager for her sons' wives to come there.

The entire day was a fog, from dressing to the ceremony in the overly crowded family chapel.

Kieran wore a beautiful tartan in the Ross colors of green and black over his shoulder and had newly shorn hair for the ceremony. Their vows had been recited, hers in a soft voice, his in a clear, deep one.

Tears had glided down her cheeks while Kieran remained composed, his features calm.

Afterward, they'd sat in front of the great room and eaten and then exited out to the courtyard to the feast prepared to feed the masses.

The familiar faces of the village vendors made her happy. Gisela spent the day moving from one group to another, chatting and laughing. It was the most enjoyable of experiences.

Preferring not to be around crowds, Kieran and several men celebrated by drinking ale at a table that was set away from the others.

It didn't bother Gisela in the least. He was acting as he always did.

When the day ended and the moon rose, Kieran came to her. Instantly, her heart quickened, and she couldn't help but let out a long sigh when he wrapped his arms around her. He was so very striking in the moonlight.

"The day I traveled here, ye promised to show me something." There was a playful light in his gaze. She would have to get used to this side of Kieran.

"Come." She took his hand and led him away from the bonfires and lanterns and around the side of the keep facing the woods.

For a long minute, she searched the skies until finding the

formation like that of an hourglass.

"Look up there at the stars. See the one there and then there…" she pointed at different stars outlining the formation. "That formation is my favorite."

Kieran looked for a moment, but then searched her face instead.

"Are ye happy, Gisela?"

Her gaze snapped to him. "Of course. This is the most perfect day. Are ye?"

"I am," he said as his brows lowered. "Is it wrong of me?"

She wrapped her arms around his waist. "If yer father were here today, would he be glad for ye?"

Pondering her words, his chest rose and lowered, the steady heartbeat reassuring in her ear. "Aye, he would," he finally said.

"Ye are allowed to be happy, Kieran. Part of life is that ye and I will one day also die. Our loved ones will continue without us and that makes me glad. I would not wish for them to mourn and miss living their own lives."

"Ye are right." He lifted her face and covered her mouth with his. Gisela clung to him as the kiss deepened. Her breath caught when his hand cupped her bottom and he pushed his hips forward, demonstrating how much he needed her.

"I think we should probably find our bed," he murmured in her ear.

Her insides turned soft, like porridge. Gisela couldn't keep from blushing when they made their way through the crowd and into the keep.

"Goodness," she exclaimed when they finally entered her chambers. They'd decided to spend their time there together until returning to Dun Airgid.

They'd been together before. He'd shown her how things were between a man and a woman and how touches and kisses brought one to a climactic point, but she knew they'd not joined in the way they would that night.

"We should undress," Gisela said, moving to the dressing

screen. "I won't be but a moment."

When he took her arm and turned her to him, she gasped. "I will undress ye."

"Is that what a married couple does?" she asked, hating how maidenly she probably sounded to him.

"If they wish, aye," he responded. Then he studied her for a long moment. "Ye are aware I have never been married either, are ye not?"

It was as if her feet floated above the floor as Kieran kissed each part of her that the clothing fell from. He seemed to sense her every thought and need, and pressed his lips to the precise point that needed attention.

"Oh," Gisela exclaimed when he lifted her up and carried her to the bed, placing her with gentle ease upon the bedding.

It did not feel strange or odd to her when she watched him undress. Instead, anticipation made her want to urge him to hurry. At the same time, she wished to commit every moment to memory and never forget what transpired on their first night as husband and wife. When all clothing was done away with, Kieran stood perfectly still, allowing her perusal.

He walked to the bed with what seemed like hesitancy. Surely he'd been with many women. She held out her hand. "I cannot wait for ye to be all mine."

Lowering his shoulders, he climbed on the bed and lay next to her. "I believe that is what I should be saying to ye."

"Then say it."

He pulled her against him and Gisela could not formulate a thought. The touch of their bodies was so new, so alluring that she had to take a hard breath. "I love ye, Kieran."

Their mouths met, hands traveling and discovering each other's bodies. He was hard and firm, while at the same time, his skin was soft. The calluses on his hands brought shivers of anticipation the more they traveled all over her.

Reason left her. And as much as she wished to cling to the here and now to remember everything, when his hand moved up her thigh to the apex between her legs, she lost control.

How was it that one tiny place on her body could bring so much enjoyment? It was a question she'd ask later. In that moment, she could only writhe with pleasure and lift her hips to his hand.

Kieran took the very tip of her breast into his mouth and his tongue emulated the movements that his fingers did between her legs.

"Oh!" Gisela cried out and sunk her teeth into his throat and pulled the skin between her lips, needing to taste him.

When he positioned himself between her legs, his darkened gaze met hers. "Ye are a wildcat."

Taking her hands in one of his, he held them above her head. "Now, lay still."

It was impossible. How could he ask that of her when remaining without moving was the one thing she could not do?

With his free hand, he guided his hardness to her sex and nudged at the entrance. "Relax and enjoy this," he admonished when she lifted her hips, wanting it to happen for him to take her as his.

His sex was hard and thick, making Gisela wonder how he would fit. She squirmed just a bit, unsure what was expected.

Then without warning, he plunged.

Gisela cried out at the stinging pain. It felt as if he'd torn her insides and tears trickled down the side of her face. "That really…h…hurt."

"I am sorry. I promise it will not be like this again." He kissed the tears away, pressing kisses along both of her temples.

They were still joined, and she wondered what else would happen. It wasn't unpleasant, but it did feel strange for him to be inside while they lay still.

Odd as it was, she wanted him to move or do something besides remain still.

"What happens now?" she asked.

"I am waiting for the pain to subside before moving," he said, his mouth next to her ear. "How do ye feel?"

"Strange. It is almost as if a man has pushed himself into me and is not moving."

For the first time, she heard it. The deep sound of his laughter. "I should do something about that."

"Perhaps ye should," she said.

And he did. He slid out and then back in, the repetitive movements fluid and steady. Their skin rubbed together with each movement, their mouths together then apart as they fought for breath.

Gisela wrapped her legs around his midsection, not wishing for him to ever move away. It was much too enjoyable after all.

The air became still and she gulped in as much as she could take because something strange began to happen.

At first, there was a strange flicker, a tiny speck in the darkness. Then it grew until becoming a huge fireball that had to be extinguished. Finally, an explosion shattered her entire reality to pieces. A delightful sensation raced over and across every inch of her body until there was only something akin to a star-filled sky.

Gisela wasn't sure if she cried out, moaned or just held her mouth open in a silent scream.

The room, the keep, the world disappeared into an abyss of twirling stars as she fought to cling to the bit of reality that was left.

Then she heard him. Kieran's hoarse cry as he, too, lost all control.

CHAPTER TWENTY-SIX

Dun Airgid: Ross Keep

GISELA WOKE TO find she was alone in bed. They'd been back at Kieran's home for a fortnight and things had changed considerably. Kieran rose early and spent days out with the archers performing his duties as brother to the laird and part of the guard.

He rarely returned before last meal. Most days, she assisted Elspeth with household duties. She helped Merida and Ceilidh in the garden and then oversaw the cleaning and mending needed for her and Kieran's personal space and clothing.

She'd never learned to sew, and it was something Gisela wasn't about to take on. Remaining still while pulling a needle through clothing seemed the most boring way to spend time in her opinion.

Instead, she procured a small room on the first floor, cleared it out and began the task of collecting herbs and flowers to make perfumed oils. Soon, she'd begin making soap. Although she'd brought quite a few with her, the women of the keep had been gifted a good portion and there was little left.

After dressing, she meandered to the great room where Ceilidh sat with Merida. Both women looked to her.

"Where is Elspeth?" she asked.

Ceilidh looked glum. "She isn't allowed to leave her chambers today. The midwife insists she is about to give birth."

"I believe a woman should be allowed to do as she wishes within the household," Merida said. "Elspeth should be up and about."

When Ceilidh leaned forward, her eyes searching the room, Gisela and Merida followed suit. "I believe this is the laird's doing. He is being overly protective, but doesn't wish Elspeth to know it is he who desires her to remain cloistered."

"I suppose we can go up and keep her company," Gisela suggested. When a maid neared, she smiled at the young girl. "Just warm cider and a piece of bread please." Then turning to the others, she explained, "My stomach is a bit upset this morning"

Merida studied her. "Please do not tell me ye are already with child."

"I have only been married for a bit over a month."

"And yer monthly flows have occurred?" Ceilidh asked with lifted brows.

Gisela rolled her eyes. "Ladies, we must come up with a way to help Elspeth escape."

She ate the bread and drank the warmed cider. Then collectively, they went up to the second floor where the laird's large chambers were.

They found Elspeth in the center of a huge bed, arms cross over her swollen stomach and a deep frown directed at a woman who sat in a chair staring at the hearth.

"We've come to give ye time to rest," Ceilidh announced to the woman who gave them a relieved look.

Merida nodded. "We assure ye, she will remain here in bed. Go on now and spend some time in the kitchen. Go out and get fresh air after ye eat something."

The woman glanced at Elspeth who growled at her and hurried out of the room.

As soon as the door closed, Ceilidh rushed to the wardrobe. "We've come to help ye escape. There is something new to see," she teased.

"What is it?" Elspeth slid to the edge of her bed, waving away Gisela and Merida who approached to help her up.

She waddled to the wardrobe and shook her head. "Never mind all that. I will wear my robe. Nobody cares to look at me now. I look like a swollen, dead fish floating on murky loch waters."

"Oh, now that ye mention it, ye do," Ceilidh said while tugging a light dressing gown over Elspeth's head. She began to tie her friend's lacings and smiled at her. "There, now ye look like a colorful, dead fish."

Despite her obvious bad mood, Elspeth chuckled. "Let us hurry. What do ye have to show me?"

"First, we shall meet the new guards," Ceilidh said.

"They are twins," Merida murmured.

"Quite handsome," Gisela added.

Elspeth's eyes lit. "Should we find them wives?"

"Of course," Ceilidh said.

"What else?" Elspeth asked as they waked out of the chambers to the corridor.

"Ian is so proud of his new shield. He wishes us to see him fight. I haven't quite dared yet, but today we shall, together."

As they walked down the steps, assisting Elspeth, they hurried out a side door so they wouldn't be caught by the midwife. Once outside, they giggled like young girls.

Gisela couldn't believe her luck, to have come to live and become family in a keep where the women were all young like her and discovering married life. Together, they would raise children, love their husbands and help the clan become better for its people.

A young lad happened by and, immediately, Merida ordered him to go fetch the twins. Elspeth also cautioned the lad not to tell a soul they were out there. Excited at knowing a secret, the lad hurried off to do as he was told.

"May I speak to ye," Merida asked Gisela. "I have a favor to ask of ye."

"Aye, of course," Gisela said, not quite understanding what she could do for the woman.

Merida pulled her a short distance away from the other two who were having a deep discussion of their own.

Gisela studied the woman. Merida was a McLeod and very proud of it. She had red hair and beautiful blue eyes. It had to have been hard for her to come to live there amongst the enemy who her own clan had battled against.

"What is it?"

Merida let out a long breath. "Yer husband, Kieran, he barely speaks to me. I can live with it, but it disturbs Tristan greatly. Everyone can sit together as brothers and wives, but when I try to join, he always walks away."

"I have noticed. I am so sorry." Gisela took Merida's hand. "I will speak to him about it."

With an obvious shiver, Merida studied her. "I thought Malcolm was unapproachable, but Kieran. Everyone found him so distant. Ye have changed him. He seems almost human now." Merida's eyes widened at her statement. "I am sorry, I do not meet to insult him or ye."

"I understand." Gisela chuckled. "He can be very intimidating."

Just then, the twin guards arrived and they joined Elspeth and Ceilidh who peppered the poor men with tons of questions.

"Are either of ye betrothed?"

"Where are ye from"

"How do I tell ye apart?"

The men took their questions in stride, obviously used to curiosity as they were identical. Gisela didn't wait for them to tell how to distinguish them. She motioned to the one on the right. "Ye, are shy and have a stronger lilt when speaking." Then she pointed to the other twin. "Ye are more outgoing and have a nick on yer left ear."

The men looked at one another. The second one replied. "I am Marcus and my father nicked my ear as he could not tell us apart as babes."

"Quite savage, poor little babe," Elspeth pronounced, looking about to cry.

The more timid of the twins met Gisela's gaze. "I didn't know I have a more pronounced lilt. I am Monroe and I lived in Ireland for a wee bit."

After being questioned for another length of time, Monroe and Marcus were finally were allowed to leave.

Just then, Malcolm and Kieran appeared.

Malcolm went straight to Elspeth. "Ye must go inside. We were informed ye were missing and I ordered guards to search for ye."

Elspeth allowed him to hug her and then pushed him away and announced that she wished to see Ian spar.

After a moment, Malcolm nodded. "Very well."

Kieran met Gisela's gaze, and his face softened.

"I must speak to ye," she called out after him.

He slowed, allowing for her to come up beside him. Ceilidh and Merida walked just behind Malcolm and Elspeth who continued to speak her case against being kept in her chamber.

"I did not know ye remained on the keep grounds today," Gisela said.

Kieran nodded. "Aye, for a bit. I am traveling south today. A group of archers are required to escort visitors who shall be arriving later this day. We must go south to meet them."

"Is it dangerous?" she asked, taking his arm.

He shook his head. "Nay, I do not believe so."

"Ye avoid Merida."

When he didn't respond, Gisela knew him well enough to know he did hear her, but preferred not to speak on that particular subject.

"She is yer brother's wife and, besides, is sweet, caring and has even tried to teach me to sew. I still hate it by the way. She wishes the family to be without animosity and because ye avoid her, Tristan is frustrated."

Still, he did not reply, his gaze straight ahead.

Gisela continued. "I just ask that ye not get up and walk away when she approaches. There is no good reason for them to have a bad day or evening because of ye. I am not asking for ye to be her friend, just that ye not be so obvious about yer dislike of her."

"I do not dislike her. It is what she reminds me of that I wish to avoid."

"I understand," Gisela said. She pulled his arm and lifted on her toes to place a kiss to his mouth.

The kiss caught him off guard. She laughed when his cheeks colored and he looked around to see if anyone was watching.

"I will try," he acquiesced.

CHAPTER TWENTY-SEVEN

GISELA JOINED THE family at the top of the stairs just past the gates as the visitors arrived. They were from Clan Urquhart, the laird's brother, his daughters and a large contingent of warriors heading north to visit Laird Sutherland.

There was to be a betrothal between the clans, which would benefit Clan Urquhart, a small clan with few affiliations.

The laird had not fathered any daughters, but his brother had two. Both were set to be married, which one depended on who was chosen upon their arrival.

Gisela was filled with pride upon the escort of archers entering the gates. Naill led the first ranks of archers. Kieran's would bring up the rear.

Once the carriage came to a stop, the Urquharts were assisted down and were greeted by Malcolm. Elspeth was inside in her chambers since she'd exhausted herself that morning.

Gisela, along with Merida and Kieran's uncle, greeted the visitors next. Once all introductions were made, they all went inside for last meal.

As they were seated, Gisela had to admit that both of the Urquhart daughters were beauties. One of them seemed shy but nice. The other was aloof, seemed to find fault in everything and was not at all likable.

The shy one, Fiona, instantly seemed to find kinship with Gisela. Fiona sat next to her upon entering. "I love this keep. It is beautiful," she whispered. "Do ye like living here?"

"I do," Gisela replied with a smile.

"Which one is yer husband," the young woman asked, scanning the room.

Just then, Kieran entered. She didn't see him, but knew by the Urquhart sisters' reactions. Both inhaled sharply, their eyes rounding. She'd yet to get used to that.

"He is my husband," she said without turning around. "The breathtaking one."

Fiona blushed. "I apologize."

"Please do not. He is quite a sight, is he not?"

The young woman had yet to look away from Kieran and she nodded. "How can ye live with it. He takes the attention of everyone in the room."

"Most days, it's just family. Some people here actually dislike him." Gisela chuckled. "Now tell me, how do ye feel about marrying soon?"

"I hope it is not me who is chosen, but it probably will be. Esme can make herself cry actual tears when she dislikes something, which men can find alarming."

Gisela looked to the other young woman who had the expression like that of someone smelling a rotting corpse.

"I am shocked she is not sobbing at the moment."

When Fiona dissolved into laughter, Gisela loved her. "If ye could spend more time here, I think we would become good friends."

Fiona nodded with enthusiasm. "I wish we would."

THE GREAT ROOM was filled with people who ate and drank ale.

The atmosphere was festive as chatter rose over music played by a very talented troubadour. People danced and jokes were told until everyone cried with laughter.

As much as she enjoyed the company of the Urquharts, the festivities continued on much too long and, soon, Gisela could barely keep her eyes open.

She bid everyone a good night and went to her bedchamber.

Moments later, the plush bedding cradled and soothed the fatigue away.

Kieran entered, his large body outlined by the fire in the hearth. He yanked his tunic over his head and threw it onto a chair, the boots and breeches followed. Bowing his back and arms overhead, the stretch of someone seated too long, he let out a loud yawn.

When he slid into bed, the smell of whisky tickled her nose. How she loved every single thing about him. One arm snaked under her and he pulled her close. The kiss, mostly on the mouth, was sweet, but short as he slurred something about a long day.

Within minutes, he was fast asleep, his arms firmly holding her in place. Gisela sighed.

Perhaps not the best way to fall asleep with her face mushed into her husband's chest. But she'd slept alone for many a night and this was as close to perfect as anyone could ever dream.

What seemed just moments later, there was loud banging on the door.

Gisela sat straight up and blinked into the darkness.

"Who is it?"

"Ye must come at once, Lady Gisela," a maid said from the other side of the door.

Kieran stirred but didn't wake. She brushed a stray lock from his face and, with a sigh, slipped off of the bed and over to the door.

"Coming," she called out, but was sure whoever it was had hurried away.

THE SCUFFLING OF feet and frantic whispers continued as everyone was filled with expectation and nerves.

Childbirth was always this way. As much as new life was anticipated, there was always the underlying fear of something going wrong.

This was the laird's wife, giving birth to the next generation in a family that had gone through many tribulations caused by a death. Gisela burst into the room and everyone turned to look. She ignored them, of course, not caring at the moment for more than following the instructions Elspeth had begged her and Ceilidh to follow.

"That water, has it been boiled?" Gisela asked a maid who walked in with two buckets.

"Pour it into the cauldron there on the fire. Go to the kitchen and boil more and then bring it along with two additional buckets." She went to a small cabinet and pulled out stack of linens that she had overseen washed and boiled in a clean basin. Then she went to the bed where Elspeth was, half-sitting up, her face wet with perspiration.

"Where's Ceilidh?" she asked.

Elspeth attempted to smile, but her beautiful face twisted as a labor pain struck. "Gone to fetch Merida."

Gisela took her hand and gave it a squeeze. "I will ensure everyone washes their hands properly. Now, let us get some clean linens under ye."

The midwife eyed them with suspicion, but followed instructions. She had been thoroughly instructed by Elspeth at least several times and yet there were no clean linens spread on the bed yet.

Merida walked in the room. She was regal, posture straight, gaze sharp. She took one look at the midwife and pointed to a chair. "Ye will not be involved in this. I am a trained healer and midwife. The only reason ye are here is because the laird asked it."

The woman who seemed more relieved than angry, did as

she was told.

After the bed was stripped and all the bedding replaced with the clean linens, Elspeth settled in for what could possibly be hours of labor. Her back was propped up with pillows and Ceilidh was instructed to sit behind her. Whenever Elspeth needed it, her back was rubbed and all three women soothed and encouraged her.

There was a knock at the door and Malcolm called out, "How is she?"

When Merida motioned to Gisela, she rushed to the doorway. Cracking it just a bit, she looked at the laird's pale, drawn face. He truly loved Elspeth, it was obvious.

"She is doing well. It won't be long now."

"Are ye sure?" he asked. For a moment, it looked as if he were going to push his way in.

"I am," Gisela said, smiling at him. "Elspeth is strong."

It was a short labor. At least it seemed to be. Gisela was sure Elspeth wouldn't agree. Perhaps two hours later, the loud wails replaced Elspeth's moans as she'd pushed hard and then harder to deliver the child.

A boy. And a hardy one by the loud cries of protest at being thrust into a strange new world.

Merida called out instructions. She cut the cord that connected the babe to its mother. Gisela cleaned the child, ensuring he was without any type of injury that would bring worry. Ceilidh assisted in the continued removal of the bloody linens after the final discharge.

The swaddled bairn was placed in Elspeth's arms and she cried in joy. Then, after everything was cleaned up, per her instructions, Merida went to the door and allowed Malcolm in.

His gaze pinned Elspeth's face, making sure she was well and not hiding something sinister that perhaps was happening to her body which was hidden under the fresh cover that had been spread over her.

Only after he was assured she was well, did he look to the

pink-faced, swaddled child.

"A boy," Elspeth said, a tear trailing down her face.

One by one, the women slipped out, allowing the family some privacy. Merida stopped just outside the door and hugged her husband who'd been waiting with Malcolm. "A boy," she said, wiping an errant tear.

Gisela noted that Ruari and Ewan were also there. They'd been waiting with Malcolm. Her husband, however, was noticeably absent.

"I will return momentarily," she said, walking to the bedchamber where she planned to dress and prepare for the day. The sun was up and it would be time to start the day soon. She was much too excited to go back to sleep.

A new life had arrived, and she'd taken part in it. Her lips curved into a wide grin. She had seen a new life brought forth and it had been…beautiful.

⟫⟫⟫⟨⟨⟨⟨

KIERAN FORCED ONE foot in front of the other. Each step closer to his brother's chamber was harder to take than the last. On leaden feet, he managed to get just outside the doorway. The corridor was empty and through the cracked door, he heard not one sound.

Looking over his shoulder, to the right and left, he was assured no one was about.

Despite the heaviness of his legs, Kieran managed to not make a sound as he made his way across the room to a bassinette where the child lay. He wasn't sure what he'd expected, but definitely not what he saw.

His heart immediately was filled with joy at the sight of the beautiful babe. A Ross through and through he was. With a slight scowl marring his tiny brow and a half-smile on his lips, he resembled Malcolm. Yes, he would be a true Ross, strong and proud.

In the bed, Elspeth slept soundly, exhausted from the delivery. The child was of a good size, which had probably cost the mother. No matter how long he lived, he would never stop marveling at how such delicate creatures could be so strong when giving life.

He slipped his hands gently under the child and lifted him up. He barely weighed a thing. The babe made a soft sound like that of a wee beast and Kieran smiled.

"His name is Robert Malcolm," Elspeth said softly.

Kieran froze. "I didn't mean to wake ye."

"I wake every time he makes the slightest sound," she said with a gentle smile and looked at the child. "Meet yer uncle, Kieran. He will teach ye the ways of a bow and arrow."

Every word she'd spoken seeped into Kieran, flowing through him like a balm. It was as if by holding the child and learning his name, the emotions that he'd held in since his father's death broke free.

At first, it was a single tear. It was followed by another and, finally, he could not hold back.

He placed the baby back into the bassinette and went to the bed. "Thank ye." A tear splatted onto the bed and Elspeth beamed up at him. "Ye are a good son, Kieran Ross. Just like I hope wee Robert will be to Malcolm."

Unable to keep from it, he nodded silently and slipped out to the balcony of his brother's bedchamber.

Kieran wept, allowing the bitterness to wash away from him. He had been sure the babe would not live or that Elspeth herself would perish. And now, along with the relief of everything going well, he realized that this child was the beginning of a new chapter in all of their lives.

One that he would do his best to ensure was as perfect as life would allow.

When he left the bedchamber, it was as if a boulder had been lifted from his shoulders. He went down the stairwell without encumberment, the injuries that had plagued him with pains in the mornings were dormant.

In the great room, people had gathered and everyone talked excitedly about the newborn wee one. Kieran went to the high board and lowered to the empty seat on Malcolm's left side.

Uncle Gregor always sat at Malcolm's right as he had before with their father.

"Did ye see him?" his uncle asked, his face stoic. Obviously, everyone was aware he had not been in the corridor with the others. Fear had kept him away and now he hated to have allowed it so much control over him.

"I did, aye. I was just there." Kieran met Malcolm's surprised look. "He is perfect. He will carry our father's name well."

His brother's eyes welled and both looked away, clearing their throats. His uncle's lips curved into a knowing smile. "Aye, he will. My brother would be extremely proud."

Gisela came up and he stood and pulled out a chair for her to sit. She kissed his jaw, her face bright with excitement. "This has been the most amazing day already," his wife declared, looking over to Malcolm. "I cannot wait to have a bairn of my own."

When Kieran choked and coughed, his brother and uncle laughed.

"Ye will make a wonderful mother to my brother's children," Malcolm said and looked to him. "My brother will be a good father as well."

Tristan and Merida entered. It was strange as they rarely joined the family for first meal. But it was a special day after all.

As per usual, Merida avoided meeting Kieran's gaze when nearing the table. She would sit on the other side of Uncle Gregor.

Next to him, Gisela stiffened. Was she afraid he'd do something to hurt Merida's feelings?

Kieran stood and pulled Merida's chair back.

At first, Merida froze and then she looked over her shoulder to Tristan who watched Kieran with a protective expression.

"Please sit," Kieran said.

"Thank ye?" Her comment sounded more like a question.

He nodded. "No need to thank me."

When he lowered next to Gisela, she squeezed his hand. "Ye are the most wonderful husband," she gushed, and a slow-moving warmth enveloped him.

It was, indeed, an amazing day as his wife had proclaimed.

CHAPTER TWENTY-EIGHT

THE CLIP-CLOP OF the horses' hooves over the cobblestones cheerfully announced they'd arrived at Kildonan. Ceilidh leaned to look out the carriage window and found that it looked pretty much the same as the last time she was there.

It was interesting that she'd expected more, not exactly sure what, but more of a festive appearance. It was her wedding day after all and Elspeth had spent countless hours with the village women instructing them on what was to be done for this day.

"Stop looking out," Elspeth demanded. She sat across from Ceilidh, holding her now two-month-old child. Her friend had not wasted time lingering in bed after the birth of wee Robert. Instead, she'd gotten out of bed within days and insisted on returning to most of her duties.

Although she spent most of her day in the chambers caring for the child, they still on occasion had gone for walks in the field and spent time in the garden.

The weather was cooler and although Ceilidh had planned a late summer wedding, it was now firmly autumn.

The burnished coppery leaves waving in the cooler air were, indeed, lovely and she had to admit they added a colorful flair to the days.

The marriage would take place in a large stable structure that the laird had ordered to be built. The village would be able to use it for gatherings during the colder seasons, so it was a welcome addition.

Once again, she peered out the window. This time, she was greeted with a view of streamers hanging from trees and windows, gaily flapping in the wind.

Her wedding day had finally arrived and by the evening, she would be Ian McElroy's wife.

UPON ENTERING THE building that afternoon, Ceilidh could barely contain her emotions. Ian, dressed in a Ross plaid, stood proudly at the front of the room, his eyes tracking her every step.

Next to him stood Kieran Ross, the childhood friends comfortable standing next to each other. Her father kept his gaze forward as he escorted her down the center of the room. But by the constant clearing of his throat, she knew he was touched by the occasion.

Her mother looked lovely in a simple gown that had been made just for her by Elspeth's seamstress.

As she walked past, her best friend in the world, Elspeth, met her gaze with happy, tear-filled eyes.

Beside Elspeth was Malcolm and next to the laird, Elspeth's father. The gruff blacksmith, along with Elspeth's two brothers and Elspeth's mother, filled the row of benches.

Her heart thundered as they finally reached the front of the room and her father stepped away. Ceilidh worried she'd not be able to hear a word.

The vows floated over the room as they spoke, eyes only for each other and hands joined, tied with a sash. If only she could freeze time and go through each moment again and again.

Was the sniffle her mother?

The murmur from behind her, was it a word of encouragement?

Who exactly cleared their throat and why?

Ian was so perfect, tall, broad-shouldered, standing before her, offering every bit of himself to her. His voice never wavered, remaining strong throughout each vow, while hers shook and, more than once, she stumbled over the words.

Finally it was done, the vicar pronouncing them joined for life and all breath left her. Ceilidh had never been so happy, so filled with joy. As they walked back down the center of the room, this time side-by-side, she swore her feet never once touched the ground.

"Ye are beautiful," Ian murmured into her ear. "My most beautiful wife."

Her heart, it was too full and felt as if it were about to burst. Ceilidh couldn't stop smiling as she looked from one familiar face to another.

The feasting and celebrating would continue into the night and then she and Ian would be joined physically. It wouldn't be their first time, as they'd been sharing the same chamber for months, but it would be different. She knew it in her bones.

Tonight would be a night they'd both cherish for the remainder of their days.

KIERAN TOOK GISELA'S elbow and guided her to the back of the room where people were gathered to wait for long tables to be assembled and the chairs arranged around them. The villagers moved with precision, which told him they'd already practiced and knew where everything would go.

Although Gisela seemed touched by Ceilidh and Ian's ceremony, she was unusually quiet. He nudged her with his arm. "Is something wrong?"

She shook her head but then looked up to him, her gaze seeming to seek an answer to an unspoken question.

"Can we step outside for just a bit. I need fresh air."

"Very well," he replied and they walked out and were greeted by cold air. Kieran pulled her close and rubbed her arm. "Why are ye so quiet?"

Children rushed out of a building and raced toward the wedding area, no doubt they'd been kept away until after the vows were said. Now, their excited high-pitched voices were allowed free rein.

Gisela followed the children's progress and then once again met his gaze. "How many children would ye like for us to have?"

The question caught him by surprise. They had many personal conversations, but it was only at night in the privacy of their chamber.

"I do not know. Five perhaps."

"Five?" Her brow crinkled. "Why five?"

So it was not the reply she'd expected. Was there a correct one? "Four then. Yes, I'd like to have four."

"Four." She seemed to mull his reply. "I suppose four is good."

"What about ye? Have ye a number in mind?" He wondered if Elspeth giving birth, which was followed by Tristan and Merida announcing they would be parents by late winter, had made Gisela think more about children.

"I think four is good," she finally replied.

His lovely wife took his hand and brought it up to her lips. "Ye have been so different lately. Although, for the most part, ye have softened, it is almost as if ye're withdrawn. I cannot explain it," she said. "Are ye unhappy Kieran?"

"No," he replied immediately. "If anything, I am happier than I have been in a very long time. With ye, I find peace and wellbeing."

"Ye had a strong purpose for each day. To go and find him, avenge yer father. But now, do ye feel the same?"

He'd not considered it but, yes, he had been restless. He missed the days of traveling, of going to the northern post or in search of finding the one responsible for killing his father. "I suppose I am a bit restless."

"Ye should find what it is that ye need to do now." She smiled up at him and all was well with his world.

"Gisela, ye are my reason for being. I suppose I should consider things I prefer. Perhaps providing escort for Malcolm and Elspeth when they go north to visit my mother."

When his wife did not protest, Kieran became bolder. "I could go to the northern post for a few weeks to ensure all is well there."

"As long as ye do not stay over long, because I would miss ye terribly. But ye cannot be away early spring."

"Early spring. Aye that would be perfect because when I go north, I will be forced to remain through the winter." There was excitement in his voice. He tried to temper it. But in truth, the idea of resuming the life he'd had, before his father's death, motivated him.

How was it that he'd been so fortunate to have such an understanding wife? "What about ye?" he asked. "Do ye wish to go back to spend time with yer mother while I am away?"

"Nay. But I will request ye bring her back upon yer return. She would wish to be here when our first child is born."

He nodded understanding that it was a special time for women.

Then the air stilled. Realization dawned and his breath caught. For a moment, it was as if the word spun and he was the only thing still. He met Gisela's beaming face and his mouth fell open.

"Ye're with child?" Each word came out stilted. "How long?"

"I have known for a few weeks. But I have been waiting to assure all was well. Ye have a hard time with loss."

"I am not a child to be coddled." Kieran scowled, and then took her arm. "Ye should not be out here in the cold. I will not leave yer side and spend the winter away. What are ye thinking woman?"

They made their way inside. He continued chastising her and

changing every plan he'd just made. There was no force on earth that would separate him from his wife. He had sworn to protect her and would do so until his dying breath.

CHAPTER TWENTY-NINE

"THERE IS NO reason why ye cannot go," Gisela repeated to her stubborn husband as she'd done for days. "I will be fine. Kieran, please go. Ye will enjoy the boar hunt with yer brothers and cousins."

It was late morning and, soon, she would go downstairs and hopefully find something to do away from Kieran. He constantly checked on her.

He looked out the window. He'd been standing there since the others had left earlier that morning. It was obvious he was tired of remaining nearby. And if Gisela was to be honest, she needed him to leave her be even if for a few hours.

"Please go."

He turned and scowled at her. "Why are ye so anxious to get rid of me?"

"Because I need to miss ye," she snapped. "Honestly, Kieran, yer overprotectiveness is overwhelming me. If I had known ye would hover like a vulture over a dead beast, I would have waited until ye left to go north and sent ye a letter announcing I was with child."

Despite his hurt expression, she burst into laughter at her statement.

"I do not find the humor," Kieran said, but he was making his way to the door. "I will return as soon as possible."

Gisela waved gaily at him and followed him down the corridor. "I think I shall go to Merida's house and sew. We are making baby dresses."

Her husband was already hurrying out the front door and she held back a chuckle.

WINTER CAME WITH the ferocity of a dragon. But instead of hot flames, frigid air blew across the Highlands bringing with it ice and snow that, although lovely, made traveling impossible.

Merida gave birth on a particularly snowy day with Elspeth as her midwife and both Ceilidh and Gisela assisting. The child, a beautiful boy, was born in the middle of the night and was promptly named Faolan Gregor Ross. Being that Gregor was like a second father to Tristan, they had already planned for the boy to be named after him.

Tristan, the giant father of the newborn, had been reduced to tears of joy, not caring that there were witnesses when doing so.

Gisela wondered if her babe was to be a boy as well. She hoped so. Kieran would be overjoyed like his brothers. Of course, if it were to be a girl, the child would be pampered and be a welcome addition to the circle of women she now adored.

Once again, Kieran did not appear with the group that awaited to hear of the birth. He had waited two days before asking Gisela to go with him to meet the boy.

Although he'd made efforts to be nicer, albeit small ones, toward Merida in the last months, she was still a bit intimidated by him.

Together, Gisela and Kieran walked into the chamber she shared with Tristan and Gisela approached her friend.

"Kieran wishes to see the baby."

"Aye, of course," Merida replied, eyeing Kieran. "Please meet yer nephew."

Kieran held the child for a long time, while Gisela and Merida drank warmed cider and chatted about what they'd do that day. It was a custom now that each of the women took turns keeping company with the one who was abed or kept to her quarters because of illness or childbirth.

Ceilidh had yet to conceive, but Gisela was sure an announcement would be made soon. The two were enamored with each other and constantly sneaking away. It was sweet to see the different ways in which each couple showed love for one another.

"I am going to the village with Uncle Gregor and Ewan today. There are rumblings of unrest. It seems the villagers have been poached upon." Kieran lowered the infant to his bed, kissed Gisela's cheek and walked out to of the room.

"That was not too unpleasant," Merida said with a grimace. "Does yer husband ever smile?"

"Not normally. He is quite stern. But he is gentle and sweet, and when he does smile, it is so very special."

Merida changed the subject. "So is Ewan to remain here permanently?"

"Aye. From what Kieran says, he has decided to stay for the time being. I believe he inherited land not too far from here, but must wait until after winter to see if it's where he wishes to settle."

"He's quite the rogue," Merida announced. "He is all the maids speak about. The man has conquered and vanquished many a heart already. It makes me wonder how he could possibly live alone on land away from family."

"It could be mostly talk," Gisela said slowly. "He was quite taken with Fiona. A shame really, as the poor girl may be married off to a Sutherland brute."

Just then, Ceilidh entered. She held a basket with freshly baked bread. "I bring bread and some sweet, freshly churned butter," she announced with a smile.

As they continued talking, Ceilidh informed them that an Urquhart messenger had just arrived.

Apparently halfway to their home, one of the elders had become ill and they'd come seeking a healer.

Both Merida and Gisela exchanged looks.

"Who returned with them?" Gisela asked. "Fiona or Esme?"

Ceilidh thought for a moment. "I am pretty sure I saw Fiona. However, everyone was hurried inside and taken to chambers to await hot baths and warm up."

When Gisela and Merida grinned, Ceilidh narrowed her eyes. "What are ye planning? I wish to be part of it. Winter lags much too long."

"Ewan." Gisela said without further explanation.

"He seemed to be taken with Fiona. Perhaps we should arrange for some time alone," Merida said.

They had no way of knowing how long the party would remain. Although it was Highland tradition for at least three days, they were probably hoping to arrive home before the weather truly made it impossible.

⊱✦⊰

KIERAN ENTERED THEIR bedchamber that night and went directly to Gisela who lay in bed writing in a journal. Her husband's shadow spilled over her and she looked up and smiled.

"My love, ye have returned." Reaching for his hand, she placed it over her barely rounded stomach. "Our child kicked quite a bit today. He or she is already strong."

With an expression of relief, he lowered and placed his lips to her stomach. "Ye will be a brave warrior."

Gisela giggled. "What if the babe is a beautiful lassie?"

"I vow to train her with a bow and arrow," Kieran replied then pressed a kiss to her stomach. He straightened and began undressing. "Why are ye still awake?"

"I was waiting for ye to return," she replied. "I wished to speak to ye about something."

Instantly, a deep scowl formed. "What is it?"

"Nothing too serious. Is Ewan betrothed?"

"Whatever ye are planning, leave me out of it. Ewan's hair will be white before he considers settling."

She pouted. "That is what yer brothers said as well. But he did seem taken with the lovely Fiona…"

"No," he said and kissed her lips. "Now, sweet wife, ye must go to sleep."

"I cannot possibly sleep now," she replied. "We have yet to discuss names for our babe."

Kieran pulled off his boots and britches, then rinsed off at the basin. He climbed into bed and pulled her against him, his body a bit chilled. Warmth seeped between them and she snuggled closer.

"Katriona?"

"Nay."

"Gavin?"

"Nay."

He nuzzled her neck and slid his hand down her back, pulling her closer.

"Lachlan?"

"I do not care for it," he replied, his tongue trailing from her neck to her shoulder.

"Clara is a beautiful name," she breathlessly.

"Nay." He pulled her skin between his teeth, nipping at just the right place and she gasped.

"Oh."

"I do not think our child should be named Oh," Kieran teased, his hand moving between her legs.

Gisela went taut, anticipation coursing throughout her body.

Before long, she became lost in Kieran's caresses, his kisses sending the surroundings to spin. He was everything. It occurred to her that, in that moment, all she wished to think of was him.

"Oh, Kieran!" she exclaimed when he came over her.

"Kieran is a good name," he replied, rolling over her, taking care not to crush her stomach.

"Say it again," he demanded as he took her fully.

"Mmmm."

EPILOGUE

CLARA ISABEL ROSS was born in the early spring. It was a long labor and Gisela had wanted to give up many times.

By the time her daughter's loud wails sounded, she could barely keep her eyes open. Needing to see the child and ensure she was healthy, Gisela fought against exhaustion until the pink-faced, swaddled babe was placed in her arms.

Kieran had not waited outside while she'd labored. Unlike his brothers, he'd burst into the room several times demanding to know why she was in so much pain. Only when Gisela ordered him to, did he leave.

At the sound of the babe's cries, he'd entered once again. This time, he remained by her side as she finished her labor.

Concern etched on his face, it was only when she held their daughter that he seemed to ease a bit.

The following morning, Gisela woke to the most perfect of sights.

By the window, Kieran was in a chair. He looked out to the sky with a soft smile on his lips. In his arms, he held their daughter and spoke to her in soft tones.

Seeming to sense she'd awakened, he looked to her.

"I was introducing Clara to Da."

Gisela's heart squeezed. "Ye must always tell her about him so that she will get to know her grandfather through her father."

He nodded and she marveled at how much he'd changed.

Kieran was no longer the hellish Highlander she'd met while selling soap in the center of her village.

The man before her was now a caring, devoted husband and no doubt a doting father as well.

Love did indeed conquer all.

The End.

About the Author

Most days USA Today Bestseller Hildie McQueen can be found in her overly tight leggings and green hoodie, holding a cup of British black tea while stalking her hunky lawn guy. Author of Medieval Highlander and American Historical romance, she writes something every reader can enjoy.

Hildie's favorite past-times are reader conventions, traveling, shopping and reading.

She resides in beautiful small town Georgia with her super-hero husband Kurt and three little doggies.

Visit her website at www.hildiemcqueen.com
Facebook: HildieMcQueen
Twitter: @HildieMcQueen
Instagram: hildiemcqueenwriter